"Thanks f**n't feel like y   d,"**

"I have the time." Graham moved next to her.

Reeny looked around. "Let me just make sure— Oh!" She'd stepped on something slippery.

Graham made a grab for her, catching her midfall. His hands clutched her arms and her hands were pressed against his chest.

He was so close. Close enough that she could smell peppermint and a subtle spicy scent she couldn't quite identify.

His eyes had a look of concern and a hint of something else she couldn't name.

"Mo-om, are we going to be here much longer?" Her son's voice abruptly cut through the fog.

Graham stiffened and stepped back.

"I think we're about done, Phillip. Why don't you start gathering up your stuff?"

Turning back to Graham, she saw he had started stacking empty boxes. She moved to help him and he glanced over. There was no hint in his expression of what had just passed between them.

Had she read too much into that heart-stopping moment, sensed a connection that wasn't real?

Books by Winnie Griggs

Love Inspired

The Heart's Song

Love Inspired Historical

The Hand-Me-Down Family
The Christmas Journey

WINNIE GRIGGS

is a city girl born and raised in southeast Louisiana's Cajun Country who grew up to marry a country boy from the hills of northwest Louisiana. Though her Prince Charming (who often wears the guise of a cattle rancher) is more comfortable riding a tractor than a white steed, the two of them have been living their own happily-ever-after for more than thirty years. During that time they raised four proud-to-call-them-mine children and a too-numerous-to-count assortment of dogs, cats, fish, hamsters, turtles and 4-H sheep.

Winnie has held a job at a utility company since she graduated from college, and saw her first novel hit bookstores in 2001. In addition to her day job and writing career, Winnie serves on committees within her church, on the executive boards and committees of several writing organizations and is active in local civic organizations—she truly believes the adage that you reap in proportion to what you sow.

In addition to writing and reading, Winnie enjoys spending time with her family, cooking and exploring flea markets. Readers can contact Winnie at P.O. Box 14, Plain Dealing, LA 71064, or e-mail her at winnie@winniegriggs.com.

The Heart's Song
Winnie Griggs

Steeple
Hill®

Published by Steeple Hill Books™

STEEPLE HILL BOOKS

Steeple
Hill®

Recycling programs
for this product may
not exist in your area.

ISBN-13: 978-0-373-87606-8

THE HEART'S SONG

www.SteepleHill.com

Printed in U.S.A.

Praise be to the God and Father of our Lord Jesus Christ, the Father of compassion and the God of all comfort, who comforts us in all our troubles, so that we can comfort those in any trouble with the comfort we ourselves have received from God.
—*II Corinthians* 1:3-4

To the members of Handbell-L, a fabulous online community of handbell ringers, and to the helpful folks of the AGEHR organization—thanks for your generosity and patience in answering all my questions. Special thanks go out to Carol Pickford, Roy Attridge, Sarah Sundin, Valerie Stephenson, Carol W. Fleeger, Katie Schlegel and Gail J Berg for their very detailed responses. Any errors that crept into this book in regard to handbell choirs are entirely due to my own misinterpretation and are not in any way a reflection of the information provided to me.

And to my brother Neil—thanks for your help in figuring out a realistic scenario for the disaster that occurs near the end of the book.

Chapter One

"So you're really going through with this."

"Yep." Graham Lockwood shoved the last box into his SUV without glancing Mike's way. He'd said all he had to say on the subject last night.

"I can't believe you're leaving without telling anyone."

Graham slammed the hatchback shut. "I told you and Carla."

"Not until last night." Mike stared at him accusingly. "You must have had this move planned for a while."

Graham only shrugged. Interviewing for this job had taken him out of town overnight twice in the past month and it appeared no one noticed. Not even Mike, who was both his best friend and his brother-in-law. Or was one still considered a brother-in-law when the connecting link was gone?

He pulled his sunglasses out of his pocket and slipped them on. Mike was too perceptive by half.

Mike hunched his shoulders. "I know you needed a break after—" his Adam's apple bobbed "—well, after what happened."

Graham's jaw tightened. Even fifteen months later, Annie's brother couldn't say the words, either.

"You can still reconsider," Mike added. "They haven't filled your position at J. T. Simmons yet. And Patty's ready to step down as the church's music director whenever you say the word."

"J. T. Simmons will find another teacher." Graham checked the backseat to make certain everything was properly secured. "As for the music director job, I meant it when I said I'm no longer interested." He hadn't set foot in a church since the funeral and didn't see that changing anytime soon.

He closed the vehicle door and forced a smile, trying to ease the tension. "Education is my vocation, but music's only a hobby."

"It's a God-given gift," Mike insisted stubbornly. Then he gripped the top of the vehicle's driver side door. "You've got friends here, Graham," he said quietly, "people who care about you. You owe them the chance to say goodbye."

"I don't want a big send-off." He'd had enough of the sympathetic looks, the everything's-going-to-be-fine speeches and the pretend-nothing's-changed conversations to last a lifetime.

"But someplace called Ten Penny Ville, Louisiana?" Mike's lips quirked up in a smile that almost looked believable. "Are you trying to hide yourself in the swamps of Cajun country?"

"It's called Tippanyville." Graham nudged his sunglasses higher with the tip of his finger. "And it's closer to central Louisiana than the southern half. As for why I chose Tippanyville— the school there needs a new math teacher and it seems as good a place as any for a fresh start." Truth be told, what he needed was a complete change of scene. Something that didn't shove unwelcome reminders in his face every time he turned around.

He straightened. Time to go. "Give Carla and the boys my love."

Mike took his proffered hand, then impulsively threw his other arm around Graham's shoulder in a quick, masculine embrace before stepping back. "Carla wanted to be here to say goodbye herself. But with Andy running a fever…"

"I know. The kids come first, and that's how it should be." Graham tried to keep his tone even, but from the flicker in Mike's expression he knew he hadn't entirely succeeded. He was glad he had the sunglasses to hide behind.

Mike stepped back and jammed his hands in his pockets. "Whatever you're looking for, we'll be praying you find it."

Graham wanted to tell him to save his breath, that he didn't believe in the power of prayer anymore. Instead he gave a short nod, closed the door and turned the key in the ignition.

Reeny Landry rolled over and glanced at the clock on the bedside table. One-thirty. If she didn't fall asleep soon she'd be worthless tomorrow. If only she could flip a switch in her brain and stop thinking about the latest setback in her handbell choir project. It was only mid-August, but the Fall festival would be here before you knew it.

She glanced at the picture of her husband that still held a place of honor on her nightstand even after three years. *Despite what your momma says, Ray, I know this is the kind of memorial you would have wanted. The choir could be a real ministry to some hurting people. And it'll be good for our own Desirée, too.*

Just when everything had started coming together, *this* had to happen. How in the world would she ever be able to replace Charlotte….

With a groan, Reeny took herself to task for the umpteenth time tonight. She'd already prayed about this and turned it over to God to deal with—she *had* to quit taking it back from Him. If she would only be patient, He would provide the answer. She just had to steel herself for the possibility that the answer might be no.

Of course, patience had never been her strong suit. Maybe *that* was the lesson He wanted her to learn in this.

How could people who didn't have the Heavenly Father to turn to deal with their troubles? She couldn't fathom—

What was that? She turned again, lifting her head. Sounded like a car turning into the driveway next door. Surely her new neighbor wasn't making his entrée into town at this hour?

There was already enough speculation in town—everybody was wondering why someone would move all the way from St. Louis to take a teaching job at a map dot like Tippanyville. Him slipping into town in the dark of night would certainly add to the tongue wagging.

Curious, Reeny threw off the covers and moved to the window, drawing the curtain back just enough to peek out. Illuminated by the faint glow of a distant streetlight, she saw the shadowy form of a man step out of an SUV, draw his shoulders back and roll his neck. Then he swatted at his arm and she grimaced in sympathy. The mosquitoes were particularly bad this year. And the bayou lining their backyards didn't help matters any.

After scrubbing a hand across his face, he turned and reached back into his vehicle, retrieving what looked like a large duffel.

As he walked to the front door, Reeny noted the heaviness in his steps. How long had he been on the road? No one arrived at their destination at this hour unless they'd been driving straight through from some distance.

Once he'd disappeared inside the house, she remained at the window, staring absently into the night. What was his story? Why *had* he come all this way when, as far as anyone around here knew, he didn't have ties to the community? Sure, *she* thought Tippanyville was a great place, but it wasn't as if it had any kind of claim to fame. Amazing, really, that he'd even heard of it. And it certainly wasn't as if Tippanyville was part of a well-to-do school district, so money wouldn't have been the incentive.

The sudden flash of his carport light switching on startled Reeny from her thoughts. A moment later Mr. Lockwood stepped outside and headed back to his vehicle. She could see him better now, though his features were still shadowed. He pulled a box out of the cargo area and headed back to the house, carrying himself with an economical precision that seemed almost robotic.

A few moments later he returned, this time retrieving a backpack and what appeared to be a guitar case. Now *that* was interesting. Was music just a hobby or—

Reeny gave herself a mental shake. What was she doing, standing here at the window like a Peeping Tom? The man deserved his privacy.

She let the curtain drop, then frowned and pulled it back again. She'd caught a glimpse of something—yes, there it was—a shadowy form waddling across his yard.

Oh dear, Dauber was out. Again. For a lazy, overweight beagle, he sure managed to escape from the Gaubert's fenced-in yard a lot.

Then she winced as Dauber decided to investigate the new resident up close and personal. Mr. Lockwood, unaware of the animal headed his way, nearly stepped on the beagle. Dauber yelped and the man stumbled, bobbling the guitar case. With an unexpected agility, however, he managed to remain upright and hold on to his load.

Her new neighbor's next move surprised her. Instead of a show of anger or irritation, he set the instrument case and bag down, then stooped to scratch the cowering dog behind the ears, for all the world as if he and Dauber were old friends. Dauber responded with a tail-wagging seal of approval.

After a few moments, Mr. Lockwood straightened, gave Dauber a final pat and retrieved his belongings. This time, however, instead of appearing coldly mechanical, he seemed merely tired and, well, solitary.

Reeny felt a tug of sympathy. She let the curtain drop, her conscience pinching when she realized she'd been spying on him, again.

Perhaps she'd make it up to him tomorrow with a nice, neighborly, welcome-to-town gesture.

Chapter Two

Reeny paused in the act of slicing into a pecan pie, her attention caught by a quick *rat-a-tat-tat* at the side door. Before she could do more than look up, however, the door opened.

"Hello," called out a familiar voice. "It's me."

"Come on in, Mom. Your timing's perfect. I just brewed a fresh pot of coffee."

"Sounds good." Estelle Perette pulled a chair out from under the table. "I can't stay long, though. The Glory Be's are meeting at my house today."

Her mother had been a member of the Glory Be Quilting and Prayer Circle since Reeny was a baby. The women got together every Thursday afternoon, rain or shine, at one of the member's homes. In addition to making quilts for local charities, the group was constantly on the look out for needs in the community. And while not always subtle, they were usually effective.

Some folks in town considered them busybodies, dubbing them the Nosy Nellies, but to Reeny they were an awesome group of prayer warriors. There had been periods in her life when their unique brand of encouragement and comfort had brought her through some dark moments.

Eight-year-old Desirée appeared in the doorway and her face lit up when she saw their visitor.

"How's my sweet t-girl doing today?" Estelle caught Desirée in a hug then pulled back and stroked her hair. "*Merci, chère,* you get sweeter looking every day. Are you ready for school to start back again?"

Desirée scrunched her face and shook her head.

The older woman laughed and tapped her nose. "Well, ready or not, you start on Tuesday."

Desirée's fingers flew as she signed out a question.

"Yes, *la p'tite,* I most certainly *did* enjoy school when I was your age." Reeny's mother followed the answer up with a conspiratorial grin. "It meant I got out of some of my chores at home."

Philip came in from outside, Buddy at his heels. "Hi, *Mèmeré.*" He gave her an I'm-eleven-and-too-old-for-this hug, then turned to his sister. "Guess what, Desi? I taught Buddy a new trick. Wanna see?"

With an enthusiastic nod, Desirée followed her brother and dog out to the backyard.

Reeny served her mother a slice of pie and cup of coffee, then went back to packing the food basket she'd been working on.

"I see your new neighbor's moved in." Her mother's voice sounded a smidge *too* casual. "Have you met him yet?"

Reeny glanced up with a smile. "Looking for something to report back to the Glory Be's this afternoon?"

Her mother merely smiled and took another sip of coffee.

Reeny laughed. "I'm afraid I don't have much information to offer. I *was* awake when he drove up in the wee hours, and I've seen him working with the movers most of the morning. But no, I haven't officially met the man yet."

"Well then, at least tell me what he looks like."

Reeny conjured up an image of Graham Lockwood in her

mind. "I'd say he's about six foot, slender build—but solid, not skinny. His hair is brown, a shade or two darker than mine, and I have no idea what color his eyes are." And the man also carried himself with authority and confidence— good traits in a sixth-grade math teacher.

"Sounds like you got a good look."

Reeny refocused on her mother and found herself being studied thoughtfully. Uh-oh, no telling what was going on in that fertile mind of hers. Time to change the subject. "I suppose you heard about Charlotte's job offer."

"Iona told me. Have you found someone else to direct the handbell choir yet?"

"No, but I spent this morning making out a list of people to talk to. I'm afraid it's not a very long list, though."

Estelle picked up her fork. "Did you think about Esi Almand?"

"She's on the list."

Reeny's mother's expression softened in sympathy. "Don't worry, it'll work out."

"I don't know, Mom. This is the third time the project has faced a setback of one sort or another." Reeny rested both hands on the counter. "I was so sure this was the right way to go—that it was what Ray would have wanted, what God was leading me to do. I even held out against Ray's mom, for goodness' sake. Now I'm beginning to wonder if maybe I was only fooling myself, pushing for this because it was what *I* wanted. I mean, the other suggestions I got were so practical. And Ray's mom *really* wanted me to fund that stone foot-bridge."

Estelle jabbed her fork into the pie, giving Reeny a stern look. "Irene Marie, don't you go doubting yourself. Yes, Lavinia's a good-hearted woman. She misses Ray something fierce, and she naturally has her own ideas of how best to honor his memory. But this is *not* her decision. Mrs. Plunkett left that money to you for a reason. She trusted you to follow your heart, to create a memorial for Ray as *you* see fit. And as Ray's widow, you owe it to him to do exactly that. Use some of that stick-to-itiveness you're famous for."

Reeny grinned at her mom's comment. "I take it that's your polite way of calling me pigheaded." But it conjured up an image of her new neighbor as he determinedly unloaded his vehicle last night, in spite of the hour and the mosquitoes. That was something else she'd gleaned from her observations—Graham Lockwood didn't seem given to laziness or procrastination.

"It's a good thing you're trying to do, *bébé*." Her mother's tone softened. "I haven't seen Joscelyn this excited about anything since she moved back to Tippanyville. And I can tell Desirée is looking forward to it, too."

Reeny sighed. "I know—and they're not the only ones I drew into this. I just hope I don't let them all down." She pushed the hair off her forehead with the back of her wrist. "Because I promised Ray's mom if I didn't have the choir up and running by the Fall Festival, I'd consider going with her idea instead."

Her mother paused, then gave her a sympathetic smile. "I didn't know. Well, you just hang in there. You still have lots of time. I'm sure the good Lord is working on someone's heart even now. And you know the Glory Be's are pulling for you. This is as important to us as it is to you."

Reeny smiled. "With the Good Lord and the Glory Be's on my side, how can things *not* work out?"

"Exactly!" Her mother gave her a that's-settled-then nod. "In fact, this project is right at the top of our prayer list."

"I appreciate that." Reeny placed a cloth over the food basket. "By the way, would you mind watching the kids for a few minutes."

"I'd be glad to." Estelle eyed the basket. "You have an errand to run?"

"Actually, I thought I'd take a meal over to Mr. Lockwood. You know, to welcome him to the neighborhood."

"Oh?" Her mother gave her another of those looks. Then a small smile twitched her lips. "How neighborly. Well, get on with you then. And take as long as you like. I'll be here when you get back."

Reeny, whose cheeks felt a bit warm, didn't doubt that for a minute.

"And," her mother said as Reeny crossed the kitchen, "you can find out what color his eyes are."

Reeny didn't bother responding as she headed out the door.

A few minutes later, she took a deep breath as she pushed Mr. Lockwood's doorbell with her free hand. Okay, so delivering meals to shut-ins was more her thing than boldly paying a welcome visit to the town's newest eligible bachelor. But then again, it wasn't often that the town *had* a new eligible bachelor to welcome. And he was her next-door neighbor, so who better to be the first to greet him?

Besides, she couldn't shake the image of how he'd looked last night as he'd stooped down to scratch Dauber's ears, like one lonely soul comforting another. It made her want to reach out and let the man know, regardless of what he'd left behind, he was welcome here.

Thinking about that little vignette also helped tame her nerves a bit. After all, a man who could make nice with a dog like Dauber would surely be at least polite when faced with an uninvited guest on his front porch.

Her lips tilted up at that thought. Naturally, he chose that moment to open the door. She felt her cheeks warm, as if her thoughts might be visible on her face.

His polite smile set her mind at ease on that score, but she noted he didn't attempt to open the screen door still separating them. "Can I help you?"

His voice caught her off guard. She'd expected the accent, of course. After all he was a transplant to the area. But she hadn't expected the deep rich timbre of it, or the way it resonated within her.

And, after another quick glance, she could now report that his eyes were a warm, weathered-cypress gray. He also had a touch of silver in his hair—giving him a distinguished look.

All details her mother would be interested in.

"Hello," she said, realizing he was waiting for her to say something. "Mr. Lockwood?"

He nodded acknowledgment, polite reserve still firmly in place. Maybe he was the sort who took to dogs better than people.

"I'm Irene Landry, your next-door neighbor." She lifted the basket she'd packed. "I thought I'd bring over some lunch as a welcome-to-Tippanyville offering."

His expression warmed a bit but now she could see the tired lines in his face. Probably hadn't gotten much sleep before the moving van arrived this morning.

"That's very kind of you." He opened the screen door. "Please come in." He grimaced as she stepped inside the front room. "Sorry about the mess—I haven't had a chance to get things sorted out yet."

"That's okay. I saw the moving van leave just a bit ago, so I'd have been surprised to find things all shipshape." Actually, the place was more orderly than she'd expected. His rather spartan furniture took up very little space and the remaining unpacked boxes were neatly lined against a far wall. If this had been Ray, there would've been a jumbled mess piled in the center of the room. Neatness hadn't been her late husband's strong suit.

She lifted the basket again. "In fact, that's why I brought this over. I figured you hadn't taken time to eat lunch yet."

His expression shifted to a smile. "You figured right. I was just thinking about opening a can of soup."

He had a nice smile. Very nice, in fact—warm and masculine at the same time. "Now that's no way to celebrate your arrival. Why don't I just unload this in the kitchen?"

"Yes, of course." He swept a hand toward a doorway to the left. "This way."

She already knew the way—she'd been here hundreds of times when the Guillots owned the place—but she let him usher her into the familiar kitchen.

Setting the basket on the red Formica-topped table, she began removing the contents. "I hope you like pork chop jambalaya. It's what I cooked up for lunch today and I made a larger than normal batch." She gave him a challenging grin as she pulled out a small red bottle and waggled it between her fingers. "I even brought you your own bottle of Tabasco sauce in case you're up to trying it the way the locals do."

He raised a brow. "Tabasco—that's a sissy form of the habanero pepper, isn't it?"

Okay, so the man had a sense of humor behind that reserve. She smiled and reached back in the basket. "There's also a couple of biscuits, some baked beans and a slice of pecan pie."

"Mmm. This isn't lunch—it's a feast." He sketched a short bow. "Mrs. Landry, you are looking at one grateful man."

A definite thawing of attitude. Must have just been exhaustion earlier. "Please, call me Reeny. And it wasn't any trouble. In fact, something you'll learn pretty quick about folks around here—we do enjoy our food."

"Well, that's at least one thing you have in common with people in St. Louis." He moved to one of the cupboards. "If you'll give me a minute, I'll dish these up so you can have your bowls back."

Thoughtful, too. "Oh, there's no need. These are disposable containers." She tucked the cloth back into the now empty basket. "Do you know about the PTA reception planned for Saturday afternoon?"

"Yep. My invitation arrived before I left St. Louis."

"Good. You'll meet a lot of your new neighbors there. But in the meantime, if you want to start mixing and mingling, Bayou Cigale Park over on the east side of town has a nice walking trail." He looked very fit, in a lean, athletic sort of way. "A lot of folks go there when the weather's nice. And Erline's Snack Shop and Gift Store over on First Street serves as the unofficial town gathering place." She grinned. "Serves pretty good milk shakes, too."

"Thanks. I'll keep that in mind."

Was that a hint of dry humor in his voice? She decided to take it as a good sign.

She turned back to the table and hooked the basket handle over her arm. "Now, I know you're still trying to get settled in so I'll leave you to it. Besides, I left Mom watching the kids and promised I wouldn't be long."

He followed her back to the front room. "So, you have children?"

"Two. Philip just turned eleven and Desirée is eight. Which means you'll have Philip in your math class."

"I look forward to meeting him. And your husband?"

It'd been a while since she'd run into anyone who didn't know she was a widow. Surprising how deeply that question could still slice at her.

She managed to keep her expression composed. Or at least hoped she did. No point making him feel bad for asking. "Ray was the high school football coach. He died in a car accident about three years ago."

That news, no matter how calmly she delivered it, was usually met with some variation of sympathy, pity and/or discomfort. *His* reaction, however, was one she hadn't encountered before.

His expression closed off immediately and his whole being stilled. Even though neither of them moved, it suddenly felt as if there was more distance between them than there had been a second ago.

"My apologies." Even his tone lacked inflection.

Maybe this was his way of dealing with awkward social situations. "No need to apologize—you couldn't have known. Besides—" she flashed a smile, trying to get things back on a more comfortable footing "—I don't mind when people bring Ray up. He was a big part of my life for many, many years and the memories are all good ones."

He made a noncommittal sound, and she cast about for a change of subject. Her gaze snagged on the corner of an upright piano sitting in the next room. Propped next to it was the guitar case she'd seen him with last night.

A small bubble of excitement stirred. She'd been too distracted last night to connect the dots, but could this be the answer to her prayer?

She waved toward the instruments. "I see you're a musician. It's a talent I've always admired." When he didn't say anything she tried again. "Is that a classic or steel guitar?"

"Classic." He didn't expand and while his tone was polite, his demeanor was charged with a definite off-limits warning.

So much for feeling him out about helping with the handbell choir.

Reeny tucked a strand of hair behind her ear and cast about for a safer topic. She noticed a bible stacked with a group of other books on a corner table—an obviously well-read one. With a smile, she turned back to him. "By the way, if you're looking for a church to attend this Sunday, I'd be glad to—"

"I'm not."

Bam! Another brick wall. She'd definitely done something to get his dander up. In fact, though his words remained civil he had a pronounced why-are-you-still-here look in his eyes.

Keeping her smile firmly in place, she moved toward the door. "All right. But if you need any pointers on Tippanyville itself—like where to buy groceries, or on the relative merits of the Cypress Knee Café versus Dominick's Seafood Grill— just let me know."

"Thanks for the offer, but the school board sent me a packet with information on local businesses." His tone hadn't softened any. "I'll probably do a bit of exploring on my own the next few days."

Okay then, she'd definitely overstayed her welcome— time to make her exit. Still, she didn't want to end the visit on a sour note. "I'd say that was adventurous of you," she said lightly, "but I'm afraid there's not much chance of your getting lost in a town the size of Tippanyville."

That earned her a stiff smile that didn't quite reach his eyes. Thank goodness she'd finally reached the front door. Maybe she should just stick to bringing meals to shut-ins in the future. "Well, enjoy your lunch. And welcome to Tippanyville."

Chapter Three

Graham watched her hurry down the steps of his front porch as he slowly closed the door. He kicked himself for being such a lout. He could have—*should* have—handled that so much better.

His petite, dark-haired neighbor had only been extending the hand of friendship after all, something he hadn't done anything to earn.

At first he'd been afraid she was a nosy neighbor—just coming over to see what gossipy tidbits she could learn about the new man in town. But the self-conscious smile she'd greeted him with, as if unsure of her welcome, had given her a touch of vulnerability and charm that had nudged aside his reservations.

He hadn't been altogether immune to her sense of humor and the air of energy and openness about her, either. There was that south Louisiana accent in her voice, too—hard to describe but it had a certain earthy, lyrical quality to it that the musician in him was captivated by. He'd found himself listening to her voice as much as her words. Yep, he'd relaxed enough to actually feel as if he'd pull off this transition to his new life with ease.

Right up until she'd mentioned the death of her husband.

That unanticipated reminder of his own loss had slammed into him like a blow to the gut. Everything she'd said after that, from pointing out Annie's piano to inviting him to church had just added to his roiling emotions. A part of him realized she was trying to put him at ease, but her words had grated anyway—it would be like mentioning the loss of a limb and then saying, "But my arm and I had good times together so I don't mind talking about it."

He raked a hand through his hair as he moved back to the kitchen, trying to exhale some of his tension as he went.

He'd overreacted, plain and simple. Not the way he'd planned to start his new life. Sure, her cavalier-sounding dismissal of her own loss had hit one of his hot buttons, but he couldn't have it both ways. Either he wanted folks to act naturally and not tiptoe around him, or he wanted folks to respect his feelings and avoid mentioning anything that triggered memories of all he'd lost.

He grimaced as it occurred to him that his reaction to the news of her husband's death had been every bit as uncomfortable as the reactions he'd left St. Louis to escape from.

Time to remind himself why he'd made this move. No more walling himself off the way he had back in St. Louis. In fact he looked forward to making friends among his new neighbors. Friends of the casual sort, of course—coworkers, neighbors, students. People he could have informal, nothing-between-the-lines conversations with, people who would stop and talk when his path crossed theirs, but who didn't probe too deeply into his private life.

He'd begun to miss those kind of interactions lately and been aware enough to know that he couldn't wallow around in his self-imposed isolation forever. But he didn't have the desire to let any relationship go deeper than casual friendship. Not with anyone. Not again.

Graham rubbed the back of his neck as he opened one of the containers his neighbor had left behind. If the enticing aroma was any indication, the woman could definitely cook.

A self-mocking smile twitched his lips as he pulled a dish from the cabinet. Probably wasn't any real danger that Reeny Landry would be looking for any sort of deeper relationship with him than that of neighbor. Especially after the way he'd just treated her. He had some bridges to mend there.

While the microwave did its thing, Graham stared out the kitchen window at the lush backyard that had played a big part in selling him on this house. A beautiful oak with sweeping branches and touches of Spanish moss filled one corner, almost hiding the shallow bayou that meandered along the rear property line. Closer to the house were a couple of wisterias that had been pruned into nice-size bushes.

Through the window screen he could hear the sound of a dog barking and children playing. It was coming from the other side of the wall of azalea bushes the separated his yard from Reeny Landry's.

The microwave dinged and he moved away from the window, snatching a fork from the silverware drawer as he went.

No, the self-appointed, one-woman welcome wagon likely presented a different kind of threat to his plan to build a quiet, well-ordered new life. He had her pegged for one of those people who didn't believe you when you said that you actually enjoyed quiet evenings at home. She had all the earmarks of what he and Annie had jokingly nicknamed YOGs. YOGs were people who justified their busybody activities by saying they were imposing whatever unwelcome intrusion on your privacy they deemed appropriate for "Your Own Good."

If he wasn't careful she'd have him roped into joining every kind of civic and social group in town and, worse yet, she'd try to pair him off with one or more of her single friends.

Yep, he'd definitely have to keep an eye on that one.

Reeny hung up the office phone and struck another name from her list. That was it. Over the past four days she'd called every name on her original list and worked up a second one that included anyone in town who had even a hint of music experience. And come up dry. She was now officially out of candidates.

So, what next? After weeks of work and prayers it looked as if she wasn't going to be able to pull this off after all. The worst part would be telling the bad news to the folks who'd believed in her and had been so excited about the project.

Especially Joscelyn. Her best friend since third grade and the current assistant principal here at Tippanyville Elementary was the one who'd been most in her heart when she'd come up with this plan.

She closed her eyes and rested her forehead on her palm. *Dear Lord, I thought I would be doing a good thing with this handbell choir project, but perhaps I was just being selfish. Is this Your way of telling me to put it aside? Or is it merely a test of my patience and faith? Please, help me to see my next step.*

The sound of a throat clearing startled her out of her thoughts and her head snapped up. Graham Lockwood stood on the other side of the desk, staring at her with a concerned frown.

She shifted, remembering their one and only conversation four days ago. Their parting after her less than successful welcome visit had been awkward if not downright chilly.

"Mrs. Landry, are you all right?"

His question and concerned tone surprised her. Seems he'd gotten over whatever had soured his milk when she'd dropped by the other day. "I'm fine, thanks. Just asking for some Heavenly guidance with a problem I'm trying to work through."

A spark of emotion flickered in his eyes, there and gone before she could identify it.

"I see." His brow furrowed slightly. "Pardon me, but I didn't realize you worked here."

Did her presence bother him? "Actually, I don't—at least not officially. I volunteer to help out now and then. Since classes start back tomorrow I thought some of the teachers and staff might need a bit of help getting things ready."

He shifted. "Oh, well, that's quite commendable of you."

She swallowed a grin at his stuffy-sounding comment. Did all people from St. Louis talk that way? "Thanks. So, is there something I can help you with?"

"Mrs. Laborde mentioned there have been a few changes to the school calendar since I received my packet. She was supposed to make a copy for me."

Agnes Laborde was the school secretary and had been ever since Reeny herself was a student here. "I'm holding down the fort while Mrs. Laborde helps Paulette with a new book order for the library. But…" Reeny walked to the secretary's worktable. "I think I saw—yes!" She triumphantly lifted a bright blue sheet of paper. "Here it is."

"Thank you." He accepted the schedule from her and turned away. But before he'd taken so much as a step, Joscelyn came bustling in from the hallway.

"Reeny—" the scratchy rasp of her voice was so at odds with her delicate, willowy features "—Mrs. Laborde asked me to tell you—"

Seeing the new math teacher, Joscelyn immediately shifted into her more businesslike, assistant principal demeanor. "Oh, hello, Graham, is there something I can help you with?"

He lifted the paper. "Thank you, but Mrs. Landry found what I was looking for." He gave them both a polite nod. "Ladies." With that, he headed out the open door and turned down the hallway.

Reeny stared after him through the large window that fronted the school's office. She couldn't quite figure the man out. He'd been polite, almost pleasant, for most of her welcome-wagon visit, then given her that chilly send-off. And just now, when he'd first walked in he'd seemed genuinely concerned about her, but he'd closed off almost immediately.

She'd seen him twice more since that first visit. While she and the kids were at the park Saturday morning she'd spotted him jogging on the walking trail. She'd watched the way his feet pounded the ground, admiring his form, wondered again at the air of isolation that seemed to encapsulate him. As far as she knew, he hadn't noticed her.

The second time had been that same afternoon, at the PTA reception. She'd nodded to him across the room, but had been more than happy to keep her distance and let those who hadn't had the opportunity to meet him introduce themselves and engage him in conversation.

She couldn't help but watch the way he interacted with the group, though. He smiled and said all the right things and mingled nicely with everyone. While his air of reserve had been duly noted, he apparently hadn't turned frigidly polite with anyone else the way he had with her. In fact, that reticence of his had, as Joscelyn put it this morning, given him an "air of mystery."

From all accounts it appeared he made a good enough impression that more than one unattached female and wannabe matchmaker had added him to her bachelor of interest list.

Even Joscelyn herself had seemed taken with—

"Quite the gentleman, isn't he?"

Reeny started and turned around to find Joscelyn eyeing her with a knowing look. Oh dear, just how long had she stood staring at the empty doorway? "I suppose." She moved back to Mrs. Laborde's desk and retrieved her notebook.

Joscelyn didn't seem in too big a hurry to head for her office. "Handsome, too."

Reeny plopped her fist on her hip. "Joscelyn Anna Dupree," she said archly, "do I detect a note of interest?"

"A woman would have to be blind not to at least notice the man." Joscelyn shrugged. "I doubt I'm his type, though."

Reeny immediately jumped to her defense. "Any man would be lucky to have you." She shrugged. "Besides, I don't think any of us know him well enough to figure out his type just yet. And anyway, love doesn't happen by type."

Joscelyn shook her head. "The same dyed-in-the-wool romantic at thirty-one that you were at thirteen when Ray Landry set his sights on you. Besides, no one's talking about love. I just made the innocent observation that Graham Lockwood is a handsome man." She waggled a pencil between her fingers. "If I was going to guess the man's type, however, I'd say *yours*—"

Reeny raised a hand. "Don't even go there. And FYI, you're way off base. I can't seem to have a two-minute conversation with the man without getting his back up over something."

Joscelyn tapped her chin for a moment. "Interesting." Then she straightened and changed the subject. "I saw Lavinia earlier. She gave me a bless-your-heart smile so I take it she knows about Charlotte's move. I hope you didn't have to endure an I-told-you-so speech."

"Actually, I haven't talked to her yet."

Her friend's understanding look prickled Reeny's conscience rather than easing it. Ray's mom taught fifth-grade history here at the school. Even though they didn't always see eye-to-eye, she loved her mother-in-law, and the two of them had had a close relationship over the years. Normally Reeny would have made time to drop by her classroom to chat for a few minutes and see if she needed help with anything. But today she'd actually been avoiding her, hoping to find a replacement for Charlotte before they ran into each other.

Which was petty and uncharitable. It was wrong to let this difference of opinion drive a wedge between them the way it had. After all, they'd both loved Ray and were only trying to do the right thing. "I'll stop by her classroom after I take care of a few other matters."

Then she gave her friend an apologetic look. "I'm still not having any luck finding a replacement for Charlotte."

"That's too bad." Joscelyn carefully straightened a few papers that were stacked on the office counter. "I suppose you checked with Donna Guidry and Howard Arceneaux."

"Yes, and Claire Davenport and Marcy Timmons and Grady Chauvin and Patty Simmoneaux—" Reeny waved her hands in frustration "—and just about anyone else I know who has ever so much as picked up a musical instrument in this town."

She flipped open her notebook, as if a new name might have magically appeared there. "There were a few who thought the whole idea of a handbell choir was a misuse of the money, but for the most part the folks I talked to had valid reasons for saying no—other commitments, extended trips, illnesses, family obligations—bottom line, no one can take the job right now." It was almost as if God was deliberately closing doors. But why?

Joscelyn made a noncommittal sound, then rallied with a tongue-in-cheek smile. "Oh well, I can always take up the rubboard and join Alton's zydeco band."

Reeny forced herself to match Joscelyn's teasing tone. "I think you'd look fetching with a rubboard strapped to you."

Joscelyn gave a divalike toss of her head, then turned serious. "You know," she said slowly, "the answer to your problem is right in front of you."

"What do you mean?"

"Direct the group yourself. You have some music training and you have the time and drive for it."

Reeny was shaking her head before Joscelyn even finished her sentence. "My music training consists of three years of high school marching band. And you know I'm more of a behind-the-scenes person than a leader."

"Says who? Trust me, you definitely have it in you to be a leader." She leaned forward, her demeanor demanding attention. "There was a time when you'd jump at a challenge like this. *Mais chère,* when we were kids, you were one of the most fearless people I knew. You hatched up all kinds of schemes that would have made some of the boys our age think twice, and you dragged me along with you, laughing away my qualms. What happened to that girl?"

"She grew up." Reeny tried to keep her tone light, flippant.

But Joscelyn refused to follow her lead. "Growing up is not the same thing as growing timid," she said. "At least it shouldn't be."

Easy for you to say, Reeny thought. After all, Joscelyn had gone off to college right after high school and then landed a job that had her traveling around the country on a regular basis. She was well educated, well traveled and totally independent.

Reeny wasn't any of those things. She'd gotten married right out of high school, and her world had been wrapped around first Ray and then expanded to include the kids. She'd never regretted the choices she'd made, but sometimes her mind wandered into what-if land.

Besides, this wasn't a new argument between her and Joscelyn. Her friend had been pushing at her to be more of a take-charge person ever since returning to Tippanyville. And Reeny always insisted that she was better suited to being the stagehand than the leading lady.

Today, though, for the first time something deep inside Reeny stirred, as if waking from a long sleep. *Listen to Joscelyn,* it whispered. *Remember that take-no-prisoners girl you used to be.*

The voice was faint, though, lacking strength. Easy enough to ignore it for now.

And with a twinge of conscience she recalled what had brought her friend back home to Tippanyville—her bout with throat cancer. How could she have been envious of Joscelyn, even for a second?

"I guess it comes down to how badly you want this to work," Joscelyn insisted. "Especially if you have no other options."

Reeny suddenly remembered those instruments she'd seen in Graham Lockwood's living room. Nothing like being backed into a corner to get the brain synapses firing again. "Actually," she said slowly, "I may have one other option after all."

Joscelyn straightened. "You've thought of someone else?"

"Maybe." Sure, Graham had acted testy when she'd mentioned his musical instruments, but he'd already gotten his back up by then. Maybe she'd just caught him at a bad time. Here was a man who could teach and who apparently had some music background. It *had* to be more than just coincidence that he'd landed literally next door just when she'd been praying for someone with those very skills.

"What do you mean, maybe?" Joscelyn was back to looking skeptical. "Not just trying to sidestep my suggestion that you take on the role yourself, are you?"

Reeny closed her notebook. "No, really, I do have someone in mind. But it's going to be tricky approaching him about it—I'll have to pick my moment. Let me think on this a bit."

Mrs. Laborde returned just then, breathless as usual. "Sorry I took so long, but Paulette had quite a mess on her hands. Anyway, thanks for watching the office for me Reeny."

"No problem." Reeny moved toward the hallway, touching Joscelyn's shoulder lightly as she passed. "In the meantime, I promised Mrs. Bourgeois I'd help her get her bulletin board decorated today."

Joscelyn waved her off. "Good luck with your new candidate, whoever he is."

As Reeny walked down the corridor, she remembered how excited Joscelyn had been about the idea of a handbell choir, how her eyes had taken on a bit of the old fire that had been so much a part of her before her surgery. It had been so hard to tell her of this latest setback, to see some of that light dim even if Joscelyn had handled it with good humor and grace.

Hang it all, she had to do whatever she could to make this work.

Even if it meant broaching the subject with her touchy next-door neighbor.

Chapter Four

Graham closed the student folder and leaned back in his chair, rolling his shoulders to ease the stiff muscles. He wished he hadn't cut his morning run short today—it made his whole day feel off.

Then his nose twitched. That was food he smelled. His stomach gave a Pavlovian growl, and he glanced down at his watch. Twelve thirty. No wonder.

He identified the aroma—pizza. Some of the other teachers must have ordered lunch in.

One glance at the rain drizzling against his window and he realized why. He should have brought a sandwich with him. Oh well, his house was an easy five-minute drive and he wouldn't melt.

Graham stood and retrieved his keys from his desk drawer. Then looked up when he heard a knock on his open door.

"Hello." Mrs. Landry stood there, a paper plate supporting two slices of pizza in her hand and a smile on her face. "You a Canadian bacon fan?"

He hesitated a heartbeat, tempted by the smell of the pizza. Hearing the tempo of the rain intensify to downpour status, he found himself nodding. "My favorite."

"Then you're in luck." She entered his office and plopped the plate on his desk. "There was a run on the pepperoni, and I didn't think you looked like a sweep the kitchen kind of guy."

And what did a sweep the kitchen kind of guy look like? "This smells wonderful. Thanks."

She handed him a couple of napkins. "You'll need these. Erline's pizzas are great, but they tend to be a bit on the greasy side."

"Most good pizzas do."

The woman grinned, accentuating the laugh lines around her green eyes. "I can tell you're a connoisseur." She waved him down. "Don't feel you need to stand on my account. Dig in."

Graham remained standing. "Have you eaten?" he asked impulsively. No time like the present to work on the social skills he'd let lapse the past year.

A touch of mischief teased the dimples back for another appearance. "Who do you think got the last slice of pepperoni?" She nodded toward the door. "I'm fixing to get a drink from the machine down the hall. Can I get you one?"

Fixing to seemed to be a local way of saying *about to*. Just one of many colloquialisms he was trying to get used to. "Only if you let me buy." He set the keys down and pulled a couple of bills from his wallet.

She accepted the money from him. "What's your preference?"

"I'm not picky, just so there's no caffeine, and it's not diet or fruity."

That earned him a raised brow. "Not picky, huh?" With a shake of her head, she disappeared out the door.

Graham sat and bit into the slice of pizza, grinning in spite of himself. Reeny Landry certainly made it hard for a person to remain detached—she seemed determined to make him feel at home in spite of himself.

"Here you go," she said, returning a moment later. "One sugar-filled, caffeine-free cola."

He took another bite, polishing off the first slice. "Thanks."

She plopped down in his guest chair and opened her own drink. Seemed he was going to have company for lunch. He wasn't quite sure how he felt about that.

She, on the other hand, seemed right at home.

"So, what do you think of Tippanyville?"

And she also didn't beat around the bush. "I haven't been here quite a week yet," he said carefully, "but I like what I've seen so far."

Her smile broadened. "I'm glad. I know things must be very different here from what you left back in St. Louis."

Which, as far as he was concerned, was one of the biggest pluses the place offered. "I was ready for a change." Someplace that didn't present memories at every turn.

She cocked her head at that, a speculative expression on her face. "I've never lived anywhere but Tippanyville. Guess I'm just a dyed in the wool homebody."

Graham refrained from comment as he raised his soda to his lips. He'd rather not get involved in a let's-talk-about-our-pasts discussion. "So, do you volunteer here on a regular basis?"

She nodded. "I'm room mother for Desirée's second-grade class."

He knew what a boon the volunteers could be to a busy homeroom teacher. "It's nice to find a parent who gets involved in her child's education."

This time she shrugged. "It's the least I can do. My daughter was born mute. The teachers here have done a great job integrating her into the regular classroom environment, and I like to show my appreciation whenever I can."

Mute? "I'm sorry. I didn't—"

She held up a hand. "No need to apologize. Being mute is just a part of who she is. And with God's grace we made our peace with it a long time ago."

God's grace? He shifted in his chair, not wanting to go down that road, either. "Well, even so, not all parents are so giving with their time."

She flashed a self-deprecating smile. "I work from home so my hours are mostly flexible. And I like being involved in my kids' lives."

"What sort of work do you do?"

"I keep the books for some local businesses." She grinned. "Seems I have a head for spreadsheets and number crunching."

Interesting. He wouldn't have taken her for a bean counter. She seemed more of a people person. Then again, he didn't really know her very well. "Sounds like a good skill to have."

She laughed. "That's one way to look at it. And yes, it's every bit as exciting as it sounds. But I get to set my own hours and work from home, so I'm not complaining."

No, she didn't strike him as much of a complainer. And thinking of her being a people person, he asked, "Maybe you could help me with something?"

She sat up straighter. "Be glad to try."

"I've been going through the student list for my classes and some of these last names are, shall we say, interesting. I need a local to help me with the pronunciations so I don't come off as a complete fool right off the bat when I call roll tomorrow."

She nodded. "Now that's something I can help with. You got a for-instance?"

"Well, I know *e-a-u-x* is pronounced like the long *o* in toe. And a lot of these are obvious—like Greene, Blanco, Richard—"

"Ree-shard."

"What?"

"Not *Richard*. It has a long *e* sound with emphasis on the last syllable. Ree-*shard*."

He groaned. "So even the easy ones aren't so easy."

She grinned sympathetically. "Don't worry, it won't take you long to figure it out. And it doesn't hurt for the teacher to appear just a little bit human to his students."

"Bite your tongue."

Reeny laughed outright at that. He decided he liked the sound of it.

"Okay, so let's look at that list." She moved next to him, slowly reading the names out loud. He tried to ignore the surprisingly distracting light vanilla scent she brought with her as he made phonetic notes next to the more indecipherable names.

"Thank you," he said once they reached the bottom of the list. "This'll be very helpful."

"No problem. After all, what are neighbors for?" Something on his desk caught her eye. "What's this?"

He followed her gaze to the abacus on the corner of his desk, part of a collection he'd started in his college days.

She reached out as if to touch it, then turned back to him. "May I?"

"Of course." He was surprised by her interest. Not many people appreciated his out-of-the-ordinary collection.

She picked it up and gently ran her fingers along the frame. The wooden beads on this one were plain polished wood but the frame was intricately carved. It happened to be one of his personal favorites.

"This is beautiful. Andrea would love it." She glanced at him with a smile. "She's a local artist who does some amazing wood carvings. I'll have to bring her around to meet you so she can take a look at this."

Uh-oh. He remembered his earlier thoughts about her

being a YOG. Was she trying to fix him up with one of her single friends?

The key ring he'd placed on his desk caught his eye. The tiny diamond set in the rocklike nugget stared balefully at him, reminding him not to go down that road again.

"Yes, well, I'm sure your artist friend has seen better pieces." He swiped his mouth with the napkin, then wadded it up. "Thanks for the pizza, it was just what I needed. Now, I'd better get back to work. Tomorrow's a big day around here and I have a lot of things to do to get ready. As you can see…" He indicated the stack of folders on his desk.

"Oh. Of course." Her expression reflected both surprise and a flash of embarrassment as she placed the abacus back on his desk and moved to the door. "I'll let you get back to it, then." She gave a half smile, one that invited him to smile along. "Imagine that, getting kicked out of the classroom at my age."

Her attempt at humor tweaked his conscience. Perhaps he *had* been a bit abrupt. Still, encouraging YOGs rarely did anyone any good.

A few seconds later, Graham leaned back in his chair as he heard her speak to someone in the hall and then the sound of her laughter drifted into the room. With a frown, he tossed the rest of the debris from lunch into the wastebasket and retrieved his keys.

The gold token brushed a cold reminder against his thumb as he slipped it back into the drawer.

He'd done the right thing in sending her on her way.

Hadn't he?

Reeny's smile faded as she moved down the hall. Graham Lockwood was more of a puzzle now than before. How could someone seem so open and friendly one minute and so shut off the next?

Maybe it was just her. Had she done or said something to irritate the man?

Whatever it was, she'd lost yet another chance to ask him to help with the handbell project. She should have been more direct—just come right out and asked him as soon as she walked in his classroom rather than trying to ease into it with small talk.

Well, the good news was, since she hadn't broached the subject with him yet, he hadn't had a chance to turn her down yet. She'd just have to come up with a plan B.

If she could only make him see how wonderfully this would minister to the community, she was certain he would agree. Besides, it would help him, too. He'd have a chance to get involved with the folks here, to be a part of the community in a meaningful way.

Reeny's steps took on a renewed sense of purpose as she continued down the hall. Yep, she'd just lay it all out for him at the next opportunity and then let God handle the rest.

Thirty minutes later, Reeny was headed toward the kindergarten wing when she met her mother-in-law in the hallway just outside the teacher's lounge.

"Hi." Lavinia gave her a bright smile. "I wondered if you were around today. How are those sweet grandchildren of mine?"

"As rambunctious as ever. Both of them are grousing about school starting tomorrow but I think they're secretly looking forward to it. Especially Desirée." Reeny braced herself for what she knew was coming next.

"I heard the news about Charlotte." Lavinia's expression was suitably sympathetic. "Any luck finding a replacement?"

She'd guessed right. "Not yet."

"That's a shame, especially after all the planning the two of you did. I know I didn't act very supportive, but I don't take any pleasure in this outcome. At least no one can say you didn't give it your all." She shook her head. "The project just seemed doomed from the start."

Before Reeny could respond, her mother-in-law patted her arm. "But better to look forward than back, I always say. Now, I know folks have been throwing *beaucoup* ideas at you, and Ray's daddy and I have heard a lot of them, too. The footbridge in the park seems like the project that'll benefit the most people. Of course, that Plunkett woman left it to you to decide, so we'll stand behind you no matter what you settle on."

It seemed Ray's mom still felt slighted by being left out of the decision making. "I'm not quite ready to give up just yet." Reeny tried to keep her tone friendly but firm. "I still have one or two more people to approach about taking Charlotte's place."

Lavinia frowned. "Reeny, I know how single-minded you can be, and I'm not saying that's a bad thing, but there's no shame in admitting defeat when life gets the best of you."

"Thanks, and I agree. But I also don't believe in giving up until I've explored all my options."

Lavinia's sigh could probably be heard three doors down. "I know your heart is in the right place Reeny, and you'll do what you think best. You always do. But, bless your heart, are you sure this really *is* what's best? I mean, a person can be so single-minded sometimes that she doesn't always see the big picture of what's happening around her."

"I only know I have to keep trying until there's nothing left to try. I pray about it every night and so far I haven't felt led to put it aside."

"I've been praying, too—praying that this all works out to everyone's good."

"And I think that's all any of us wants." She gave Lavinia

the brightest smile she could muster. "I'm supposed to be delivering this to Ms. Meyers over in the primary wing so I better run."

As Graham exited the teacher's lounge, he exchanged greetings with the frustrated-looking woman headed inside. She was one of the faculty members here—Lavinia Landry. He remembered her name because when they'd been introduced he'd wondered if she was related to his neighbor.

He hadn't intended to eavesdrop on their conversation but they'd been standing right outside the open doorway so it had been impossible not to. What had caught his ear was the hint of strain in Reeny's voice, an undertone of tension that made her sound oddly vulnerable. Strange how that had tugged at him.

Since Lavinia had asked about her grandchildren that probably meant she was Reeny's mother-in-law. The discussion must have been related to some sort of family squabble.

Not that it was any of his affair.

Still, he couldn't help but be the tiniest bit curious as to what could have made his heretofore cheerful, overzealous neighbor sound so defensive.

"That's the last of 'em," Joscelyn said. "Thanks for the help but isn't it time you headed home?"

Reeny glanced at the wall clock as she handed her friend a stack of collated documents. Two-thirty. "Goodness, I hadn't realized it was so late. Mom'll be looking for me to pick up the kids so she can head over to Lettie's."

"Then why are you still here?" Joscelyn made a shooing motion. "You know how Lettie gets when folks show up late for their beauty appointments."

Reeny laughed as she reached for her tote bag, patting it out of habit to make certain her notebook was there. "You know as well as I do that Lettie's all bark and no bite." With a waggle of her fingers, she headed toward the exit.

Remembering her encounter with Lavinia, she felt her spirits sag. It really bothered her to have this disagreement between the two of them. Why couldn't Ray's mother understand what she was trying to accomplish?

As she stepped outside, Reeny lifted her face to the now-clear sky, pushing away her gloomy thoughts. Purposefully ignoring the muggy heat, she quick-stepped toward her car, avoiding the puddles dotting her path, very conscious that her mother was waiting on her. She knew her mother enjoyed having the kids over, but Reeny didn't want to take advantage of her generosity.

The sight that greeted her when she neared her vehicle, however, stopped her in her tracks. A flat tire. Just what she needed to cap off her day.

Stifling a groan, she pulled out her cell phone and punched in her mother's number.

"Hi, Mom."

"What's wrong?"

Her mom could always read her, even over the phone. "So sorry, but it looks like I'm going to be late. My car has a flat."

"Do you want me to call Rory over at the garage to come change it for you?"

"No, I can handle it. I just hate that I'm messing up your appointment at Lettie's."

"Don't you worry about that." Her mother's voice had that same soothing tone she'd used when Reeny came in from play with a scrape, whether to her knee or to her pride. "I'll just take Philip and Desirée with me, and you can pick them up at the beauty shop when you get done."

"Thanks. I'll get there as quick as I can."

Reeny shoved the phone back in her tote, popped open the trunk of her car and tossed her bag onto the front seat.

Dragging out the jack, she was grateful, not for the first time, that Ray had insisted on teaching her to be self-reliant when it came to things like this.

She glanced at the pavement, wet and streaked with muddy run-off. Oh well, no point in being squeamish—it was time to channel her inner tomboy. She'd barely gotten the jack positioned properly when she heard the sound of footsteps behind her.

"Need some help?"

She didn't have to glance up to know who'd asked that question. His voice was unmistakable. What was with this guy? Practically throwing her out of his classroom one minute and offering to change a flat for her the next.

"I think I've got it, but thanks for the offer." She gave the jack handle a forceful pump for emphasis.

Ignoring her, he reached into the open trunk and dug out the spare tire and lug wrench. She continued to pump on the jack handle, doing her best to ignore him.

Still, it was hard to ignore the fact that he didn't have any papers or books with him, so he hadn't been on his way home. Had he come out here specifically to help her?

But how had he known—

She glanced toward the building. Of course—his classroom faced this section of the parking lot.

"This really isn't necessary," she said, moderating her tone to something a bit more friendly. "That rain earlier managed to make a dirty job even sloppier, and the damage is already done to my jeans." She brushed the hair out of her face with the back of her hand. "No point both of us getting dirty. Besides I'm perfectly capable of…"

"I'm sure you are." He leaned the tire up against the side of the car and stooped down next to her. "But my grandmother would roll over in her grave if I stood by and watched while a lady changed her own tire. She was a real stickler about these things. Besides, a little mud doesn't bother me. That's what laundry detergent is for."

The man could actually be quite charming. When he wasn't glaring icicles at her, that was.

Then she had an inspiration. "I tell you what." She leaned back, resting her hands on her thighs. "I'll let you help, *if* you allow me repay you by having you over for supper tonight."

She saw the hesitation in his eyes and mentally held her breath, wondering if she'd pushed too hard. Especially after he'd made it clear he wasn't particularly interested in having her hang around him.

But then he smiled. "Forcing me to take payment for a job I already planned to do for free. Quite a negotiator."

She grinned, allowing herself to feel a bit of hope. "It's an acquired skill."

"All right. It's a deal."

Thank You, God.

Reeny stood, giving him a smile. "Then, Sir Galahad, the job is all yours."

Chapter Five

Graham knocked on his neighbor's carport door, still not certain if this was such a good idea. Besides his general wariness of the woman herself, he had a niggling feeling that she had an ulterior motive for inviting him over. Her smile had seemed just a tad *too* bright when she issued her invitation.

He only hoped he didn't walk in to find that one of her single girlfriends was joining them, as well. For some reason, which he didn't care to examine too closely, he didn't much care for the idea of her fixing him up with someone else.

He smiled as he remembered how she'd stubbornly refused his help in changing her flat until he agreed to this arrangement. Reeny Landry seemed to be a fiercely independent woman. And he'd seen some signs of that in her daughter as well when he'd met the sprightly eight-year-old this afternoon.

His hostess opened the door, a large cook spoon in one hand. "Hi. You're right on time. Come on in and close the door before the mosquitoes spot the opening. I'm just fixing to set the table."

As soon as he stepped inside, enticing aromas, wrapped

up in the unique warmth generated by a family kitchen, greeted him. "Something smells delicious."

She pointed the cook spoon as if it were a scepter. "Compliments like that will earn you an extra portion when the bowls are passed." She studied the platter he held. "What have we here?"

"Brownies. Couldn't come empty-handed—another stricture from my grandmother."

"You really didn't have to do that, but God bless your grandmother. She sounds like a lady after my own heart."

She would probably have liked you, as well. He shook that thought off and gave her a diffident smile. "It's definitely not in the same league as that pecan pie you brought me the other day, but I've been told I make a mean batch of the stuff."

"You won't find any complaints from this crew. We're all big chocolate fans, no matter what form it comes in." She nodded toward the counter that separated the kitchen from the dining area. "Just set them over there and make yourself at home."

He studied the place settings at the table. Only four. So no one else was coming. His spirits rose.

"Sweet tea or milk?" she called out from across the kitchen.

"Tea."

She pulled out a container of each and set them on the counter. "Desirée tells me she met you this afternoon. I hope she didn't intrude."

"Not at all." Reeny's daughter had squeezed through the bushes separating their backyards, on the trail of her dog who'd apparently decided to investigate the new neighbor. The child had been a bit shy at first, but when Graham made it clear he understood sign language, her face split into a delighted grin and she began "chatting" with him as if they were old friends. They'd talked about dogs mostly, her extolling

Buddy's virtues and him telling her about Champ, the Dal-
matian that had been his own childhood companion.

Annie, a special-needs teacher who'd had a warm place in
her heart for each of her students, would have loved this little
girl.

"She also told me you know how to read sign," Reeny said,
pulling his thoughts back to the present.

There was a question in her statement. One he decided to
ignore. "Yes. My skills are a bit rusty, though. To be honest
it was all I could do to keep up with her."

"Well, apparently you did a good job." She didn't press
further, handing him a large bowl of rice instead. "Could I
impose on you to set this on the table while I get the cheese
bread out of the oven?"

"Of course."

He returned to find her setting the freshly sliced bread on
an oval platter. Once that was done, she lifted the large pot
that still sat on the stove.

"I hope you don't mind if I serve this straight from the
pot," she said. "It stays warmer longer that way and is easier
than trying to pour it up in a serving bowl."

"I'm all about making it easy." He reached for the pot.
"Here. Let me take that."

"Thanks." She handed it over to him to him, then turned
to fetch the platter of bread.

Once they'd deposited their respective burdens on the
table she nodded her head toward the hallway. "Come on in
to the family room and I'll introduce you to my son."

Graham followed her down the hall and into a room filled
with overstuffed furniture and overflowing bookcases. A boy
and girl sat cross-legged on the floor, focused on a board
game.

As soon as they realized they were no longer alone, both
children popped up.

"Philip, Desirée, Mr. Lockwood is here." Reeny turned back to him, waving to each child in turn. "You've already met Desirée. And this is Philip."

The boy stepped forward in a very man-of-the-house manner. "How do you do, sir?"

"Quite well, thank you."

While Desirée was instantly recognizable as Reeny's daughter—a miniature version really—the boy must take after his father. His hair was a sandy color, his nose was straighter than his mother's and he had a stockier build. The only thing he seemed to have in common with Reeny were his clover-green eyes and olive complexion.

"Supper's ready," Reeny announced. "You two wash your hands and join us at the table." She nodded in his direction. "By the way, Mr. Lockwood's brought brownies for dessert."

With an "Oh boy" from Philip and a face-splitting grin from Desirée, the two scrambled from the room.

A few minutes later they had all settled into their seats, and Reeny turned to her son. "Philip, I believe it's your turn to ask the blessing."

Graham bowed his head with the rest of them, feeling like a hypocrite as he did so.

"Dear Lord," Philip began, "thank You for providing this meal and for the nourishment it provides to our bodies, and thank You for the one who cooked it. And especially thanks for getting Mr. Lockwood to bring those brownies. Amen."

Graham's lips twitched at that. When he looked up, he saw Reeny trying to hide a smile, as well. Apparently she hadn't been kidding about what a hit chocolate treats were around here.

The spicy gumbo, made with a mix of shrimp, crab and sausage, was every bit as delicious as the aroma had promised. The conversation flowed freely during the meal, ping-ponging seamlessly from one subject to the next. Surprisingly, Desirée held her own.

Graham was almost sorry when it was time to push away from the table. It had been quite a while since he'd found himself able to relax at such a gathering. "Thanks for inviting me over—the meal was delicious. I'll have to jog a few extra laps in the morning but it was worth it."

He stood. "But for now, about all the activity I can manage is to help with the cleanup."

"Oh, that's not—"

He stopped her protest with a raised palm. "I insist."

She hesitated for a fraction of a second, then smiled. "Another of your grandmother's dictums?"

"Exactly."

"In that case…" She turned to her children. "You heard him, kids. Mr. Lockwood is taking your place with kitchen duty tonight, so you can go back and finish your game."

Not needing to be told twice, the pair quickly excused themselves and, grabbing the last two brownies from the platter, raced back to the family room.

His hostess carried the rice bowl to the kitchen while he followed with the gumbo pot.

"I'll get the water started in the sink and dish up the leftovers if you'll clear the table," she said.

"You don't use your dishwasher?"

"Nope." She flashed him a challenging grin. "Does that make you want to renege on your offer?"

"Not at all. I'm just surprised."

She set the stopper in the sink and turned on the tap. "Actually, I use the chore as a way to spend more time talking with my kids."

"I see." He was finding a lot to admire in Reeny Landry.

As they worked, he heard her humming softly. He didn't recognize the tune, but the sound wrapped around him like a homemade quilt on a chilly night, warm and comforting. A moment later she stopped abruptly, and he caught a self-conscious look flashed his way.

He almost told her not to stop on his account, but thought better of it. Instead, he deposited the last load of dirty dishes in the sink, then he turned to watch her slide the last bowl into the refrigerator. "That's all of it."

"So, as my guest, I'll let you choose whether to wash or dry."

Graham rolled up his sleeves. "In that case, I'll wash."

A few moments later, as she began to rub the first of the clean plates with a drying cloth, she cleared her throat. "I have a confession to make."

"Oh?" Confession had a much too personal ring to it. Something told him that, whatever it was she had to say, it was going to destroy this hearth-and-home mood that had settled around them.

"I had a reason, besides thanking you for your help I mean, for inviting you over here tonight."

"I see." He was surprised by the stab of disappointment that pricked at him. He'd begun to believe he'd been wrong and this had just been a friendly gesture for its own sake.

"I have a favor to ask, and it involves music."

Music? His music had become a personal release—not something to be shared with others. Might as well nip this in the bud "Mrs. Landry, I—"

"Please hear me out. I realize it's quite an imposition for me to be asking a favor when we've only just met, but believe me when I say I'm not doing so lightly. Just let me first give you some context for what I'm about to ask."

He hesitated, more certain than ever that he didn't want to hear whatever it was she had to say. But he'd just dined at her table, and good manners dictated he hear her out. They did not, however, dictate that he agree to do what she asked.

He gave a short nod.

"Thank you." She took a deep breath. "A few months ago I came into an unexpected windfall, an inheritance of sorts. There were some strings tied to the money, however, stipulations that I spend it for something that would serve as a meaningful memorial to my late husband. I got lots of suggestions from family and friends when word got out, but in the end I decided to use it to form a community handbell choir."

A handbell choir as a memorial? Seemed an odd choice. And hadn't she said her husband had been a high school football coach? That made her choice seem stranger still. Unless… "Was your husband a musician?" Annie had had the voice of an angel and she was a talented guitarist, as well.

Reeny laughed. "Not even close. Ray couldn't carry a tune in a bucket, though that never stopped him from trying."

He noticed the tender smile on her face when she spoke of her deceased husband. But there was no grief, no anger or bitterness. He wasn't sure if he resented or envied her the peace she'd obviously made with her loss. Maybe both?

It didn't help that he was quite aware that neither emotion was particularly edifying.

She set the plate in an upper cabinet and reached for the next one. "As for playing an instrument—Ray's focus was on other things. But he did appreciate music—all kinds." She shot a quick glance his way. "I know it seems like a strange choice. In fact you wouldn't be alone if you thought so. A lot of folks here in Tippanyville think there are other, more traditional and appropriate memorials I could have chosen."

He remembered that conversation he'd overheard between Reeny and her mother-in-law. This must have been what that was all about. He had to admit, he could see Lavinia's side in this.

But he still wasn't certain why she was discussing this with him. "I would never presume to question your decision," he said carefully. "But if you're trying to recruit me to be a member, I'm afraid—"

Her head shake interrupted him. "No. I mean, that's not the favor I'm after. In fact, I targeted some very specific people to recruit as members for this choir."

Another interesting choice of words.

"Joscelyn Dupree for one."

"The assistant principal?"

Reeny nodded. "Surely you noticed how raspy her voice is?" At his nod, she continued. "It wasn't always that way. She developed throat cancer a while back. The cancer's been in remission for the past year, praise God. But it left her with the voice you hear now." She gave him a bittersweet smile. "The thing is, music has always been a big part of Joscelyn's life. She had a voice that could make you cry for the sheer beauty of it. When we were in school she always took the lead role in any musical productions the drama department put on and she's always participated in her church choir. Just about broke her heart when she had to give it all up."

He made a sympathetic sound, but refrained from comment. That news certainly cast the assistant principal in a new light.

"There's also Geralyn Vedros," she continued. "Have you met her yet?"

He shook his head.

"Lovely woman, about three years younger than me and as sweet and perky as they come. She was head cheerleader in high school and was always such a graceful dancer. She took over Miss Shirley's dance studio and children's theater company here in town after she graduated high school. Her little troupe would put on dance recitals every Christmas and Fourth of July—the whole town showed up for them. Then last August she had an accident. She walks with a leg brace now." Reeny's expression had softened in sympathy. "She made the statement once that she felt a big part of who she was died in that accident." She paused, meeting his gaze. "I know a handbell choir won't give her her dancing back, but it might allow her another outlet for her creative energies."

So this was what she meant by targeting "specific people" for her choir. The woman was definitely a YOG—but a YOG with a heart for the hurting.

"Of course, I have a selfish reason for wanting this, as well." Her tone was almost apologetic. "Desirée. She can't speak, but she loves music as much as her daddy did. Playing an instrument such as this would give her a voice, at least in a roundabout way."

Graham found himself nodding. Annie had talked about how well her students, no matter their disability or need, responded to music.

"There are others this could minister to also," she continued, "but I think you get the idea. Anyway, I've even secured a place to practice. The local florist has agreed to let the group use the vacant shop adjoining hers."

He rinsed the suds from a glass and handed it to her. "Sounds like you have things well in hand." When was she going to get to the favor she wanted to ask of him?

"It was beginning to look that way. Unfortunately, the project suffered a minor setback last week." She grimaced. "Actually, more like a major setback. Charlotte Connick, our volunteer choir director, received a fantastic job offer and is moving to Baton Rouge. I've checked with everyone I can think of, and no one is able to take on the job right now. If I don't find someone to step in soon I'll have to pull the plug on the whole thing."

Choir director? No way. "Mrs. Landry—"

"Reeny."

"Very well, Reeny, if this is going where I think it is, I'm afraid—"

She didn't let him finish. "I know it's presumptuous of me to even ask, especially since you hardly know me, but please tell me you'll at least pray about it before you give me an answer."

That was one promise he couldn't make. "Even if I wanted to do this," he ignored her wince, "I'm afraid I know absolutely nothing about handbells."

"Neither did Charlotte. She's a pianist, though, and felt confident she could learn." She took the next dish from him, her expression earnest. "We contacted a wonderful woman with the state handbell association, and she's been very helpful and encouraging. She provided all sorts of learning resources and tips for getting started. She even put me in touch with a choir director in the area who's promised to help us, as well."

He felt the full weight of her near-pleading gaze. "Surely there's someone else—"

She shook her head. "You're my last hope."

Way to put pressure on a man. He'd been right to be wary of this one. Not just a YOG with heart, but a YOG with a cause. The most dangerous kind.

Graham pulled the stopper from the sink and turned to face her fully. Logic and reasoning were his best weapons. "You said no one could take it on *right now*. This is obviously important to you, but surely that means it's worth waiting for. I understand how impatient you must be, but I imagine within a few months you'll be able to recruit someone else to help you out."

She shook her head. "I don't have that much time."

He crossed his arms. "What's the rush? Did your benefactor put a time limit on you?"

"No, but I put one on myself."

Why would she do that? She didn't strike him as a fool-hardy woman. "I don't understand."

She took a deep breath, then exhaled. "I told you not everyone agrees with my choice on how to spend the money. One of the more vocal opponents is Ray's mother. She'd like to see the money used for something altogether different. And she can be quite persuasive."

From what he'd heard this afternoon, Reeny had done a good job holding her own.

"Ray was her only child, and she would dearly love to see a more traditional, tangible memorial. It just seemed so unfair not to let her have some kind of say in this. So I compromised and asked her to give me until the end of October to get this choir up and running and to demonstrate how wonderful a memorial it will be. And in the meantime, we would both place it in God's hands. If it fails, for whatever reason, I promised to consider other suggestions."

Looked as if she'd painted herself into a corner all right. But that was her problem—not his. Time to be firm. "It sounds like your heart is in the right place and I'm sympathetic to the situation you find yourself in. But I just don't think I'm your man. I'm starting a new job in a new town and I have no idea yet what sort of time I'll have available for extra curriculars." He winced inwardly when he saw the deflated look in her eyes.

She carefully placed the last glass in the cabinet, not meeting his gaze. Then she seemed to rally. "Charlotte is coming over Wednesday afternoon to drop off all the information and training materials she's collected, and to help me figure out the next step. Why don't you at least meet with us before you make a final decision?"

He resisted the urge to grit his teeth. The woman just didn't know when to give up. She was forcing him to be blunt.

But before he could form a firmer, absolutely unequivocal refusal, Desirée ran into the room.

Rather than approaching her mother, however, she stopped in front of him, holding out a sheet of paper. He took it from her and studied the picture of a rather ungainly dog, white with black spots. The word *Champ* was penciled above the picture in big block letters.

He looked back at the little girl and found her staring up expectantly. "Thank you," he said. "It looks just the way I remember him. I'm going to find a special place to hang this."

Desirée gave him a broad, toothy grin, signed a quick "You're welcome" and raced back out of the room.

Graham looked at the picture again, feeling oddly touched by the child's gesture. Then he glanced over at Reeny to find her staring at him with gratitude in her eyes.

"Thank you for treating her gift with kindness," she said softly.

The Landry females were definitely a force to be reckoned with. With a mental sigh, he caved in. "I suppose it wouldn't hurt to sleep on all this before I give you my final answer. What time is this meeting Wednesday?"

Chapter Six

Reeny fought the urge to chew on her nails as she waited for Graham to show up Wednesday afternoon. What had he decided? If he still intended to turn her down she might as well cancel her order for the equipment and start sifting through the other ideas folks had offered up.

Had she said enough? Should she have told him the stories of the other members she'd recruited, who had a stake in this choir?

Not everyone understood what a special ministry this undertaking could be, but her instincts told her Graham might. Because under that reserve she sensed a man who cared about people. It wasn't logical, but there it was. Her gut told her that under that reserved exterior was a caring, Godly man.

She absently nudged a picture frame about a centimeter to the left. After all, a grown man who would unashamedly quote his grandmother's teachings had to have both confidence and heart.

Please God, he has to say yes.

Coward that she was, she'd asked him to come over thirty minutes before Charlotte was due to arrive. If he was going to turn her down she'd rather it be just the two of them.

Reeny glanced at the clock on the mantel. There was still five minutes to go before he was officially late.

I know, Lord, I need to work on increasing both in faith and patience. I should just take comfort in the knowledge that the matter is all in Your hands now. She caught herself on that thought and amended it. *It was* always *in Your hands.*

The *rap-rap-rap* of a knock on the carport door rescued her from further self-examination.

When she opened the door, Graham stepped inside and returned her greeting without hesitation. Surely that was a good sign. At least he didn't seem poised to make a hasty retreat.

After the initial niceties were out of the way, she snagged her notebook off the counter and escorted him into the front room.

"Where are Philip and Desirée?" His tone was casual, matter-of-fact.

Reeny, on the other hand, was ready to dispense with the small talk and get the answer to the will-he-or-won't-he question. But she reined in her impatience. "Philip is across the street playing with Robby Ormond," she said, trying to match his tone, "and Desirée is out in the backyard on the swing."

He merely nodded, and try as she might, she couldn't read his expression. The man was downright inscrutable.

Finally they were seated, him on the couch and her on the love seat across from him. She set her notebook down and waited for him to speak.

"First, let me apologize for taking so long to reach a decision."

"It's okay." Especially if he gave her the answer she was hoping for. "I know I put you on the spot." She gave a self-deprecating smile. "I've been told I can be a bit pushy, though I prefer to think of it as focused."

He smiled at that. "Focused is a good word. I suppose you want to know what I've decided."

Was he deliberately drawing this out? "The suspense is killing me."

That earned her another smile. "An honest woman." Then he sobered. "I understand why you want to do this and how important it is to you, and to your daughter. And I agree it's a wonderful project, one that could enrich any number of lives."

Reeny clasped her hands tightly in her lap. Even though his words were promising, she could sense a *but* coming.

"But I still don't think I'm the right man for the job."

And there it was. Reeny tried not to let her disappointment show. She'd been so sure when he walked in that he would say yes. "I understand." She stood, ready to usher him out of the house so she could have time to collect herself before Charlotte arrived. "Thank you for taking the time to really think about it. I appreciate you—"

He waved her back down. "Hold on—I'm not finished. I *don't* think I'm the right man for the job of director, but that doesn't mean I'm not willing to lend a hand."

Hope flickered back to life.

"Since you find yourself in a tight spot," he continued, "I could probably swing working with your group over the next few weeks." He raised a hand, forestalling her thanks. "I said probably. Before we take this any further, tell me, what role do *you* plan to play in this choir of yours?"

His question caught her off guard. "Well, I suppose I see myself as the group organizer and general gopher. I'll take care of the equipment, the scheduling, logistics, refreshments and things like that." She waved a hand to indicate the et cetera part of her job.

He didn't join in her smile. "Sounds like a cop-out to me. I thought the choir was something you were passionate about."

She stiffened. "I *am* passionate about it. I just figure someone needs to take care of all the behind-the-scenes stuff. And organizational skills are a strength of mine."

"I don't doubt that for a minute, but I'm sure we can find someone else to handle that end of things."

Why was he going on about this? He seemed almost put out. "Maybe. But I don't see why we would need to. I'm perfectly suited—"

"Because *you* are the one who has the passion for the project, and *you* need to be a very visible part of the group. Hiding in the background sends the wrong message."

She stiffened. "Hiding? I beg your pardon, I was doing nothing of the kind. I was merely—"

"Do you read music?"

His interruptions were getting annoying. "Yes." She waved a hand, dismissing his question as irrelevant. "I played flute for three years in my high school marching band. But—"

"Ah, so you actually play an instrument, too." His smile reminded her of a cat who'd cornered a mouse.

"That's what I said. But I haven't touched it in years—"

He again ignored her attempt to explain. "That's settled then. You can direct the choir and I'll assist."

Whoa. That was some leap he'd just made. "Hold on. Playing flute in a marching band fourteen years ago in no way qualifies me to take on the job of choir director."

"Why not? Didn't you say you'd talked to everyone you could think of who'd had *any* kind of musical background?"

"Yes, but—"

"How about Charlotte? Does she have choir director experience?"

"No, but Charlotte's been playing piano since she was twelve. And—"

"What about me? You saw some instruments in my home,

but do you have any reason to think I have more than a casual knowledge of music?"

"No, but you do play a couple of instruments and you have a teaching background."

"Still, you don't really know what I can do music-wise, yet you're willing to trust me with this position rather than take it on yourself."

She didn't have an answer for that.

"You can't have it both ways. Either someone with your level of musical skill can handle the job or they can't."

"But you just said you were willing to help." She barely kept the wail out of her tone.

His expression remained less than sympathetic. "And I am. As your assistant director. You step up to the plate and take responsibility for *your* dream, and I'll help when and where I can. At least until you feel comfortable going it solo."

Reeny felt like a catfish who thought he'd found lunch only to end up on the wrong side of a hook. Try as she might, she couldn't come up with another argument to counter with.

But could she really direct the group herself? Just the thought of it put knots the size of oyster shells in her stomach.

Then again, Joscelyn had said the same thing just yesterday. Perhaps someone was trying to tell her something. Whatever the case, the only other option was to throw in the towel.

And that was no option at all.

Taking a deep breath, she met his challenging look and nodded. "Okay, you've made your point. I'll do it." As soon as the words left her mouth, she felt her stomach start to churn. What had she just agreed to? She couldn't—

"Good. In that case, you have yourself an assistant director."

Unaccountably, his look of approval warmed her, eased

her nerves, if not her uncertainties. Maybe, with him lending a hand, she could actually pull this off.

Heavenly Father, this is not the answer I was looking for, but I'll try not to question Your infinite wisdom. I freely admit right here and now that there is no way I can do this on my own and any success we have will be of Your doing. Just help me not to let the choir members down.

Feeling calmer, she smiled. "Thanks, and welcome to the team."

Graham watched the play of emotions cross her face during their conversation—relief, consternation, dismay, irritation, self-doubt and finally acceptance. Did the woman know what an open book she was? Why was she so reluctant to take on the role in the first place. Was it just lack of confidence? Or something else? Still, he couldn't help but admire her willingness to step up to the plate despite her obvious reluctance.

But her current calm assurance puzzled him after her earlier protests. Did she really understand his ground rules? "Just so we're clear, I'm only agreeing to assist, not direct the group."

She nodded, her smile self-deprecating. "I understand, and I apologize if I sounded quarrelsome earlier. Being as you're new to both the town and the people involved, I think you're being more than generous. And I promise not to take advantage of that generosity—" her grin took on a slightly impish quality "—at least not any more than I have to."

Graham shifted, uncomfortable with her gratitude. "Yes, well, before I can be of any help, I'll have to get up to speed on the instrument. I've heard handbell choirs perform before, but I've never actually touched the bells myself."

"Charlotte knows more about the hands-on aspects than I do. She should be here any time now."

Her expression remained calm but he detected an undercurrent of nervousness in her tone. Was she having second thoughts?

"In the meantime," she continued, "let me give you a little more information on where we stand."

He leaned back, giving her his full attention.

"The practice location I mentioned last night is a small building next to the flower shop. It used to be a hat shop but it's been closed for years. Ms. Wilma's given us free use of the place so long as we handle any maintenance needs ourselves."

Did she realize how much she used her hands when she spoke? The energy just seemed to bubble out of her.

"I've already had the utilities put in my name and done some clearing and cleaning," she continued. "I've also done a bit of furnishing—a microwave, coffeemaker, folding chairs, a second-hand refrigerator—that sort of thing. The structure itself is in great shape and I think it'll be perfect for our needs."

She *had* been busy. "Is there anything I can help with?"

"Thanks, but it's pretty much ready. Besides, I didn't recruit you to do the manual labor."

Definitely not a lazy woman.

"I've also ordered the bells and equipment," she continued. "Everything should be here before the end of the week."

So the money was already spent. Add optimism to the list of her virtues. Or was it more a vulnerability?

"So far I've recruited eight members." She tucked a stray tendril behind her ear. "I told you about Joscelyn, Geralyn and Desirée last night. Then there's Carrie Fontenot, Dana Gleason, Andrea Dufrene, Clotile Rabalais and Ada LeBlanc."

He wasn't familiar with any of those names. "What kind of music backgrounds do they have?"

"Mixed. Geralyn, Miss Ada and Miss Clotile have piano

training, and Miss Ada and Miss Clotile also sing in the choir. Joscelyn and Carrie both know how to read music, though neither plays an instrument. Desirée has no music training, and neither does Andrea that I know of. I'm not sure about Dana."

"Sounds like our work is cut out for us."

She waved a hand. "They're all eager to learn. As for other basic info, Desirée is the youngest at eight, Dana is seventeen, Andrea, Geralyn and Joscelyn are roughly my age, Carrie is in her early forties, and Miss Clotile and Miss Ada are sisters and in their sixties."

Obviously homogeneity wasn't one of her goals. "Do you think they'll work together well?"

She nodded decisively. "Absolutely. And Miss Ada and Miss Clotile will help in that department. They're members of the Glory Be's and joined the choir mostly to pitch in and show support, bless their hearts."

He'd learned southern women used the phrase *bless their hearts* in one of two ways—either affectionately, or to preface a backhanded compliment with a spoonful of honey. From the fond smile on her face he figured in this case it was the former.

But what was that other thing she'd said? "Glory Bees?"

"Oh, sorry. Officially they're the Glory Be Quilting and Prayer Circle. Eight of the most opinionated, somewhat eccentric, quietly selfless women you'll ever meet. You probably already know some of them. In addition to Miss Ada and Miss Clotile, there's Iona Whitney, Vergie Colvin, Ruby Plaisance, Wilma Gleason, Menette Andrus and my mom, Estelle Perette."

Only two of the names sounded familiar. "Iona Whitney, she's a first-grade teacher isn't she? And Ruby Plaisance—is she the librarian over at the public library?"

Reeny nodded approvingly. "Right, on both counts. Sounds like you're getting to know the folks around here already. Anyway, you'll run into the others soon enough— you can't be in Tippanyville for long without getting to know the Glory Be's. Miss Ada and Miss Clotile run the antique and craft store up on the highway. My mom is a retired nurse. Miss Menette is a retired schoolteacher. Miss Wilma is the florist who's giving us the use of her facility. And Miss Vergie, well, Miss Vergie never had a paying job as far as I know but she's always been the first to step up when things needed doing around our church and our community."

She tsked. "But here I go, running on again. We were talking about the choir members, not the Glory Be's."

He hadn't minded, it was fascinating hearing how her mind worked. "I notice you didn't mention your son?"

"Philip? No. In case you didn't notice, all of the other members are female. He's now got it in his head that handbell choirs are for girls. For an eleven-year-old boy that's a deal breaker. My fault since I didn't recruit any guys."

"Well, it's not all girls any longer."

She furrowed her brow, then nodded. "Oh. You mean you. I don't think that's going to change his mind."

"Beg pardon." Had he just been insulted?

"What I mean is, you'll be helping direct, and only on an as-needed basis. Philip won't see that as quite the same thing as being a choir member."

Her words bothered him, though he wasn't quite certain why. He'd already figured the as-needed part would be pretty much every session, at least for the first month or so. Not that he'd tell her as much.

"Anyway, I'm going to try to find a couple of guys to round out the group before our first practice session. That way, if Philip decides he wants to participate, he'll feel comfortable doing so."

Her powers of persuasion being what they were, he wouldn't be at all surprised if she pulled it off.

The doorbell rang before he could respond, and Reeny popped up from her seat as if the bell had triggered a hidden spring. "That must be Charlotte."

Charlotte Connick, it turned out, was an energetic blonde who couldn't be a day over twenty-six and who wore heavy, dark-rimmed glasses that should have made her look nerdy but didn't. When Reeny made the introductions, Charlotte graced him with a smile that could have dazzled the sourest of men. "So you're the guy who's going to step up and direct this group."

"Nope." Graham watched her smile falter as she turned a puzzled look Reeny's way.

Reeny shot him a thanks-a-lot look before turning back to Charlotte. "What Graham means is that he's agreed to *assist* the new director." She took a deep breath, then spread her hands. "Me."

"You mean *you're* going to direct?"

Graham frowned at her surprised tone, especially when he noticed Reeny's almost imperceptible wince. "Her enthusiasm and commitment will make her a great director, don't you agree?"

Reeny's face reddened, but Charlotte rallied quickly.

"Absolutely." Then Charlotte's smile broadened. "I suppose that's one way to make sure your director doesn't slink off and leave you in the lurch again."

Reeny, her self-consciousness apparently forgotten, patted her friend's arm. "Nobody thinks you're slinking off. This is a great opportunity for you, and you'd be crazy not to take it."

"Thanks." Charlotte slipped the tote bag she was carrying off her shoulder. "Let's get to it then. Where can we spread this stuff out?"

"The dining table will probably be best."

As Graham followed the ladies into the dining room he

wondered again at Charlotte's reaction. From what he'd seen of Reeny it was obvious that she was both a genuinely caring people person and a competent, take-charge, stubborn-as-a-bulldog-with-a-bone go-getter. In essence, the perfect combination of leader and cheerleader that a group like this needed.

Graham studied Reeny, wondering again at her earlier hesitation to take the reins. She didn't strike him as someone who was timid or afraid of a challenge. Was he wrong when he sensed the innate strength and leadership quality in her?

Once in the dining room, Reeny grabbed a notebook from the counter while Charlotte emptied her bag. The former director pulled out a binder, several CDs and DVDs, some books, catalogues, pamphlets and even charts.

Graham picked up one of the books. "Looks like you did your research."

Charlotte opened the binder. "Actually, I can't take the credit—Reeny had most of this already pulled together before I agreed to help out. Made my job a whole lot easier."

So she'd done everything short of taking on the role—another piece of the puzzle that didn't quite fit.

"Okay." Charlotte's tone was businesslike. "Let's go over all we've got here, and then I'll answer what questions I can based on what I've picked up so far."

Graham leaned back in his chair, deliberately putting distance between himself and the two women. He wanted to make sure Charlotte understood that Reeny would be running the show from here on out.

And that Reeny understood it, as well.

However, it wasn't long before he found himself leaning forward and asking questions, adding his own two cents when pros and cons of how to proceed were discussed. The world of handbell music seemed both familiar and foreign to him, a combination he found intriguing.

Finally, Charlotte leaned back and gave him a thoughtful look. "I must say, you seem to have more than a passing knowledge of how to get a choir up and running. Have you done this before?"

He hesitated a moment, casting a quick glance Reeny's way. She wasn't going to like his answer. Then he gave a mental shrug—so be it. "I minored in music while I was in college, just because it was something I enjoyed back then. When the small church we—I—attended needed a new choir director, I stepped up and served for a time." He gave a self-deprecating smile. "I eventually had to drop it when it got to be too much." Too much joy, too much worship, too much of a celebration of the faith he no longer had.

From the corner of his eye he saw Reeny sit up straighter, an I've-been-had expression on her face.

Charlotte, unaware of the undercurrents, beamed. "Choir director experience—that's perfect. Why in the world didn't you say so to start with?"

Because he didn't want the star role in this little project. "As I said, I haven't done anything like this in a while."

Charlotte brushed his words aside. "It's like riding a bike. Goodness, I feel much better about abandoning Reeny now that I know she'll have such experienced help."

She stood and Graham and Reeny followed suit. "I think I've told you everything I know on the subject. I'm not leaving for a few days yet. And even after I move, my cell number won't change. If either of you want to do more brain-storming, feel free to call."

"You know I will." Reeny escorted her to the door. "I really appreciate all you've done."

Charlotte gave her a hug. "Thanks. There's a big part of me that's going to miss seeing this handbell choir get off the ground. It's a good thing you're trying to do, and I just know it's going to become a real blessing to the community, whether they all believe it or not." She stepped back and waved to Graham over Reeny's shoulder. "Enjoyed meeting you. You two are going to make a great team."

Graham managed not to wince at that. He had the distinct feeling that his "teammate" was about to give him what for.

And he was actually looking forward to a bit of verbal sparring with her.

Chapter Seven

Once Reeny closed the door behind Charlotte, she turned to Graham, ready to get some answers. "A college minor in music and church choir director experience, huh? That's quite a résumé." She didn't bother to hide her indignation.

"If you say so."

"You deliberately withheld that bit of information from me."

"Yes."

His mild tone only amplified her feeling of having been manipulated. "In fact, you led me to believe you had only casual knowledge of the instruments I saw in your home."

"I was trying to make a point."

What point? That he didn't think she was taking a big enough part? This wasn't about who got credit for what. It was about giving the group the best chance to succeed. He had all the right skills, she didn't. If she could just—

"Don't even ask." Apparently he had anticipated her next words. "I stick by my earlier stand on where I draw the line." He raised a brow. "A little bit ago you seemed to think it was a generous offer."

His words took the wind out of her sails. She sighed. "I just want what's best for the group."

"And that's why you'll make a good director." His tone made it plain he wasn't going to budge.

It would be useless to argue further. What's done was done and she'd have to make the best of it.

So she changed the subject. "What are you doing Saturday?"

A small crease appeared between his brows. "No particular plans." His tone was cautious.

Worried she was going to try to rope him into something else was he? "Good. A few weeks ago, back before I knew Charlotte would be leaving, I arranged with a choir director over in Lafayette for the two of us to visit for the day. She's offered to provide hands-on training, allow us to attend a practice session with her group and to answer any questions we have."

"And you'd like me to go in Charlotte's place?"

"If you don't mind. I can try to reschedule if Saturday isn't convenient."

"No need. Saturday's fine." He rubbed his chin. "I'm curious. Since it appears you've already spent your money, what did you plan to do if my answer had been no?"

"God would have provided another way. He's always faithful to answer our needs." She smiled. "Of course, I suppose His answer *could* have been no. In which case I would have returned the equipment for a refund and moved on to another plan."

She saw something flicker in his expression and then that impression of walls going up returned. Is that what pushed his hot button—talk of God?

He moved toward the door. "Well, I'd better be going. We can figure out the logistics for Saturday later."

Why the sudden rush to leave? "Thanks again for agreeing to work with me."

He brushed aside her thanks. "Nonsense. I wouldn't have

agreed if I hadn't wanted to do it." His smile returned. "It'll be interesting trying my hand at a new instrument."

"By the way," she said, testing the waters a bit, "I attend services at Mt. Calvary over on Iberville St. Our choir director is always looking for folks willing to serve as fill-ins when he has to be away. Since you have experience, I know he'd love to add your name to his list, if you're interested in keeping your hand in, that is."

"Thanks, but no."

"Oh. Of course. You don't go to Mt. Calvary do you?"

"No." A small muscle in his jaw twitched, then he shrugged. "I don't attend any church here."

She wasn't ready to let the subject drop. "I guess, with you only arriving a week ago, you haven't had time to visit any of our churches—"

He cut her off. "It's not an issue of time." He jammed his hands in his pockets, and she heard the sound of change jangling. "Just to be clear, I have no plans to join any church here."

Nothing ambiguous about that. Of course, one didn't have to be a regular churchgoer to be a Christian. "But you do believe in God." It was more statement than question.

He made an impatient movement with his hand. "Of course." His tone was terse, his expression just short of angry. "But let's just say He and I are not on speaking terms any longer."

What had happened to shatter this ex-choir director's relationship with God and the church? It must have been something terrible. She gave his arm a quick touch. "He's always willing to speak—and to listen."

His expression remained stony. "Look, the matter is personal, and I'd just as soon not go into detail, if you don't mind. I just wanted to be up front with you. If my not going to church affects your decision to have me assist with the choir, I'll understand."

She was more certain than ever about her choice. "Of course, I still want your help."

He gave a crooked grin. "That desperate, huh?"

Lifting her chin, she locked gazes with him. "That sure you're absolutely the right guy for the job."

He looked taken aback by that. Which served him right after all the grief he'd given her this afternoon.

"Just so you know," she added, "the choir we're going to visit on Saturday is associated with the Enduring Faith Church there in Lafayette, and the church's music room is where we'll be meeting."

He frowned at that, but nodded. "No problem."

Why did she not believe him?

After he left, Reeny headed outside to check on Desirée. It was more habit than worry. Her daughter wore a silver whistle on a cord around her neck at all times so she'd have a way to call for help if needed. Sure enough, Desirée was happily swinging away on the tree swing Ray had hung for the kids six years ago.

Reeny plopped down on a patio chair, still trying to sort through all she'd learned about her neighbor today.

Graham was part of her choir now. And, it seemed he needed healing as much as anyone else she'd recruited— perhaps more so.

She'd been right about God's having placed him in her life at this specific time for a reason.

But apparently not for the reason she'd first thought.

Chapter Eight

Reeny gathered up her tote bag and turned to Mrs. Bergeron. "Are you sure you don't need me for anything else?"

Desirée's teacher smiled and waved her on. "No, you go on. Thanks for your help." She turned to her students. "Let's all give Mrs. Landry a nice thank-you for helping us with show-and-tell this morning."

There was a resounding chorus of "thank you, Mrs. Landry" from the twenty-one second graders.

With a wave to Desirée and her classmates, Reeny left the schoolroom. Instead of heading for the exit, however, she stepped inside the main office.

Joscelyn looked up as soon as Reeny tapped on her open door, a welcoming smile lighting up her face.

"You busy?" Reeny asked.

Joscelyn set down her pen. "I'm due for a break. Come on in."

Reeny plopped down in one of the chairs. "Just thought you'd want to know that, as of yesterday afternoon, we now officially have a director for the handbell coir."

"*C'est bon*—I knew you could do it. Your mysterious new lead paid off then."

"Yes and no."

Joscelyn raised a brow. "Mysteries wrapped in mysteries."

"My 'new lead' as you called him would only agree to assist. He insisted I take on the role of director myself."

"And you agreed? *Chère,* whoever this person is, I like him already."

Reeny made a face at her.

"Well, give." Joscelyn came around her desk and leaned on the front edge. "Who's this smooth talker who managed to convince you to take on the role when none of the rest of us could?"

For some reason she suddenly felt self-conscious. "Actually, you're the only other one who tried," she said evasively.

At her friend's raised brow she blurted out, "It's Graham Lockwood."

"I see." Joscelyn crossed her arms. "That persuasive, was he?"

"Actually, it was more a matter of being backed into a corner. His was the last name on my list and when he offered to help only if I'd take the lead, I didn't have much choice. Besides," she confessed, "I also figured if he was willing to assist, he might eventually agree to take it on."

Joscelyn shook her head, a stern frown on her face. "People don't believe me when I tell them there's a devious streak hiding inside that demure exterior of yours." Then her smile returned. "Whatever put you in mind to ask our new math teacher to direct the handbell choir? Not exactly an obvious choice."

"I saw a piano and a guitar in his home when I first welcomed him to town." Reeny shifted in her seat. "I thought maybe his arrival was a sort of divine intervention."

Joscelyn nodded. "I agree—most definitely divine intervention. We now have a director *and* an assistant director when we had neither before." She crossed her arms. "So, where do we go from here?"

"Graham and I are going to Lafayette on Saturday to meet with a choir director there and get a little hands-on instruction."

"Road trip, huh? Sounds like it might be fun."

Reeny rolled her eyes. Interesting, informative, maybe even productive, but this was strictly a business trip, not a pleasure outing.

The bell rang, marking the end of the second period and Reeny moved toward the door. "Gotta run. I want to catch Graham and talk to him before his next class starts."

With a twitch of her lips, Joscelyn moved back to her seat. "By all means. Don't let me stop you."

Reeny angled her way through the crowd of youngsters filling the hallway. When she reached Graham's classroom she found him erasing the chalkboard. To her surprise, there were no children present.

"Hi there. Got a minute?"

He turned, setting the eraser down and dusting his hands. "As a matter of fact, it's my free period."

She stepped inside the room. "I won't keep you long. I just wanted to let you know the delivery company called this morning—the handbells and equipment will arrive around three-thirty today. I plan to pick up the kids right after school and head directly over to the shop." She lifted a hand. "Not that you should feel you have to tag along—I just wanted to let you know what was going on."

He reached for a pen and paper. "I'm glad you did. I'm curious to get a better look at what I'm getting myself involved in. If you'll give me directions…"

As Reeny gave him the simple directions, she told herself the spark of pleasure she felt was due entirely to this sign of his interest in the choir, nothing more.

* * *

Later that afternoon, Graham parked his SUV on Third Street, right behind Reeny's Accord. As he climbed out of his vehicle he studied the building that was apparently the handbell choir's headquarters. A faded sign with the barely legible words *Lena's Fine Hats & Ties* hung above the door, giving away its former purpose.

But there were also plenty of signs that it had been given new life. The windows were scrupulously clean, large planters on either side of the door held colorful blooms, and a cheerily decorated welcome wreath hung inside the glass-fronted door.

When Graham entered, an old-fashioned shop bell jingled, announcing his presence. A nice touch for a handbell choir's practice hall.

Reeny, who sat on the floor tugging on packing tape, looked up and smiled a welcome as she swept her arms in an expansive gesture. "Isn't this great? I feel like it's Christmas."

She definitely looked like a kid on Christmas morning—surrounded by boxes and packing materials, face flushed with excitement and anticipation.

"Appears you made quite a haul." Still smiling at the picture she made, Graham glanced across the room and spotted Reeny's two kids situated on stools at a counter. Textbooks and notebooks were scattered across the surface in front of them.

"Hi Philip, Desirée."

The little girl hopped down and offered him a peppermint.

"Why, thank you." He started to tuck the piece of candy in his pocket, but with her eyeing him so closely, changed his mind. Her smile as he popped it into his mouth made him glad he had.

"Mom says you're going to help with this handbell choir of hers." Philip's tone reflected doubt and a hint of censure.

Did the boy disapprove of the choir or of Graham's

helping? "That's right—just to get things rolling. After all," he added for good measure, "the adventurer in me couldn't pass up the chance to try my hand at something new."

Philip's expression changed to surprise and then uncertainty.

Satisfied he'd given the boy a new way of looking at things, Graham took a minute to study the room. The only furnishings that remained from the hat shop days were the counter and display case where the kids sat, and a set of built-in floor-level cabinets and upper shelves on the wall opposite the entrance.

Had Reeny cleared out the other furnishings or had it been stripped when the previous owner closed shop?

The new purchases she'd mentioned before had been used to set up a small kitchenette-type area near the counter. Then, on the opposite end of the room from the counter sat three long rectangular tables, obviously new. And in the far corner of the room he spied a television with a DVD player sitting on a wheeled cart.

Yep. She'd been busy.

He turned back to Reeny and waved toward the tables. "Did those come in today with the rest of this stuff?" At her nod he frowned. "You should have waited until I could help you."

She dismissed his concern with a flick of her wrist. "They were pretty easy to manage. But I *could* use your help opening these boxes. Don't suppose you have a box cutter on you?"

"No, but I have a pocketknife in the SUV. Be back in a sec."

As he fetched the knife, Graham mulled over Reeny's easy acceptance of his spiritual state. It seemed the admission he'd made yesterday about not being on speaking terms with God hadn't changed her attitude toward him—at least not in any way he could see. From all appearances she was still as open and friendly with him as she'd been at that very first visit.

Which was puzzling, given how close her own relationship was with God—obvious even to someone who'd been around her as little as he had. Maybe she was one of those who had a to-each-his-own philosophy. But somehow he didn't think so.

Stepping back inside, Graham stooped down and made quick work slitting open the box in front of Reeny.

She eagerly pulled it open. "Oh, good—the table pads. There'll be tablecloths in here somewhere, too." She popped up, carrying one of the pads over to the tables.

Graham plucked up another one and followed her. As he spread the pad out on the table next to her, he nodded toward a group of boxes prominently set to one side. "Chances are, those are the bells themselves, you know."

"I know." Her expression turned sheepish. "I'm saving the best for last."

He raised a brow. "I'll just bet you were that kid who saved the chocolate rabbit in her Easter basket until all the jelly beans, peeps and marshmallow eggs were gone."

She batted her eyelashes with an overly innocent smile. "Isn't that how everyone does it?"

He shook his head, rolling his eyes.

Reeny found the tablecloths next. While she covered the pads and tables, fussing to get it just so, Graham slit open the remaining boxes on this end of the room.

She rejoined him and dug into a box that contained binders. When she moved on to a box of gloves and cleaning cloths, he pulled out one of the binders and examined it. Sure enough, they were the special music binders that also served as stands. He'd used something similar in college.

"How'd you figure what to order?" he asked. "I assume you didn't just throw darts at a catalog."

She laughed, admiring how the cloth glove looked on her hand. "I did quite a bit of research. And the folks with AGEHR were really helpful."

"AGEHR?"

"American Guild of English Handbell Ringers. They're a national association whose mission is to support and educate handbell choirs across the country. Their official motto is Uniting People Through a Musical Art. A wonderful sentiment, don't you think?"

"Seems to mesh nicely with your own vision."

That won him a surprised smile. "So you *do* understand what I'm trying to accomplish."

Of course he did. It was why he'd agreed to do this in the first place. Among other reasons.

Rather than answering, Graham nodded toward the last of the boxes. "Looks like we're down to the chocolate rabbit."

She rubbed her hands together in anticipation. "Shall we?"

Graham used his knife to carefully cut open the first of the boxes, then he lifted out the instrument case nestled inside and carried it over to the nearest table. He stepped aside with a flourish. "I believe the honor goes to you."

She took a deep breath, then opened the case as if it were a pirate's treasure chest. "Oh. They're beautiful." She reverently stroked the gleaming metal portion of the largest bell with a fingertip. "Kids, come see."

Did he detect a slight tremble in her voice? Her excitement was endearingly childlike. Smiling, Graham left her and her kids to admire the bells while he unpacked the rest of the cases.

As he set them on the table, she ceremoniously opened each in turn, seeming as delighted with the last as with the first.

Finally she shooed the kids back to their homework and looked around. "I can't wait for the rest of the group to see all of this. After our rocky start, it'll be a real boost to their spirit."

"And when do you plan to do that—show it off to everyone, that is?"

"I thought I'd set up a meeting for Sunday afternoon," she answered. "That way we can report on our trip to Lafayette at the same time. Unless you won't be available Sunday."

"Sunday's fine." Just another day as far as he was concerned.

Reeny heard that hint of hardness creep into his tone. Was he even aware he did that? Biting her lip, she turned to study the cabinets and shelves.

"I suppose my next step should be to figure out how to organize and store everything." She tried for a casual tone. "Thanks for all your help, but don't feel like you need to hang around—I'm sure you have other things to get to."

"I have time." He moved next to her. "The lower cabinets look deep enough to hold the instrument cases."

That hard edge was gone from his voice now. Had she just imagined it earlier? "I agree. And the binders and instructional materials can go up on the shelves." She looked at the remaining boxes and pulled out her notebook. "The gloves, cleaning cloths and polish ought to fit in the cabinets, too. We'll leave them in the cardboard boxes for now but I'll make a note to pick up some clear plastic bins as soon as I can."

By the time she'd written her note, Graham was already at work shelving the binders. She crossed the room and snagged one of the folding chairs. She grabbed an empty box and caught his attention as she set it on the seat. "Any paperwork you come across—packing slips, warrantees, care manuals, whatever—set in here so it'll be all together." She reached for her pen and notebook. "I'll add a file box to the shopping list and organize it all later."

They worked well together and in surprisingly short order had everything put away. Reeny dusted her hands and looked around. "I think that's it. Let me just make sure— Oh!" She'd started forward as she spoke, but stepped on something slippery.

Graham made a grab for her, catching her midfall.

"Are you okay?" he asked, worry deepening his voice.

"Yes, I mean—" Her eyes locked on his and suddenly her breath caught in her throat. His hands clutched her arms near her shoulders and her hands were pressed against his chest.

He was so close. Close enough that she could feel his breath on her face. Close enough that she could feel his heart pounding into her palms. Close enough that she could smell chalk dust and peppermint and a subtle spicy scent she couldn't quite identify.

His grip felt strong and supportive and safe. His eyes had a look of concern and a hint of something else she didn't try to name.

For a forever-long minute she forgot what she'd started to say.

"Mo-om." Philip's voice abruptly cut through the fog.

Graham stiffened and stepped back.

Taking a deep breath, she tried to get her scattered thoughts under control as she turned to her son. "What is it?"

"Are we going to be here much longer? Robby wanted me to come over this afternoon to play basketball." Was there a hint of accusation in her son's gaze?

Studiously avoiding looking toward Graham, she nodded. "I think we're about done. Why don't you and your sister start gathering up your stuff."

Finally turning back to Graham, she saw he had started collapsing the empty boxes and stacking them in a neat pile. She moved to help him and he glanced over. There was no hint of what had just passed between them in his expression—nothing reassuring or awkward or even apologetic. He merely offered a polite smile and continued what he was doing.

Had she read too much into that earlier heart-stopping moment, sensed a connection that wasn't real?

Confused, she found a large empty bag and started collecting the loose debris. "The rest of this can be carted off to the city Dumpster over by the fire station."

"I'll load it in the back of my SUV and take care of it on my way home."

"All right. Thanks." She hated the stiff, stilted tone that had crept into their conversation, but was at a loss as to how to counter it.

There was, however, one other thing she needed to ask him. Squaring her shoulders, she decided to just come right out with it. "About that deadline I mentioned the other day—you know, proving this is a viable undertaking by the end of October."

"Yes?"

"Well, I'd just as soon we not mention that to the rest of the group. It won't really serve any purpose, after all. I mean, we're going to come together and make this work or we're not. Either way, I'd just as soon not put any added pressure on anyone. This is supposed to be about support and fellowship."

He studied her a moment, then nodded. "It's your show."

She fought back a wince at that. "Thanks. Oh, and I'll have a key made for you as soon as Vicknair's Hardware Store opens in the morning. That way you can come and go whenever you please."

Another nod and then he straightened, lifting an armload of folded cardboard. "I'll start loading this up."

She watched him go, still feeling the warmth where his arm had grasped her, still feeling the beat of his heart under her palms, still feeling that intense connection when their gazes had locked. Surely it hadn't all been her imagination.

Had it?

Graham pulled up next to the Dumpster. He rubbed the back of his neck in frustration as he headed to the rear of the SUV. What in the world had just happened?

Nothing. Absolutely nothing. He'd just acted on instinct, saving her from a bad fall. Nothing more, nothing less.

His reaction to holding her could be easily explained by the extra adrenaline pumping through his system. And so what if he'd felt a rush of protectiveness—surely he'd have felt the same for anyone under the circumstances.

As for what he'd felt when her gaze locked on his and he'd heard that unexpected hitch in her breathing—

He shook his head, pushing that image away. He still loved Annie—still owed his loyalty to her and her memory.

The main thing right now was to make certain Reeny didn't read anything more into what had happened than was truly there.

Otherwise it would be a long uncomfortable drive on Saturday.

Chapter Nine

"So, out of all the schools in the country, how did you end up picking Tippanyville Elementary?"

Graham ignored Reeny's question for the few seconds it took to complete the turn onto the main highway that would take them to I-49. Though she'd offered to drive, he'd insisted on taking his SUV, asking her to navigate instead. He was always more comfortable when he was in control.

The awkwardness he'd thought might creep into their interactions after what had happened the other night had failed to materialize. Instead of reassuring him, for some reason that left him feeling off balance and a bit on edge.

He tried to shake it off, wondering if he'd read more into her reaction than had been there. After all, it had been over in a matter of seconds.

"I was looking for a change of scenery," he finally answered. "And Tippanyville seemed as good a place as any."

"But how did you even find us? I mean Tippanyville's little more than a speck on the map and it's well off the beaten path. Not a place you'd just stumble upon unless you were actually looking for it."

"There's an online database that lists available teaching

jobs all across the country." He'd spent quite a bit of time studying it, looking for something to spark some excitement in him again. "This particular opening was one of the positions that met all my criteria."

She raised a brow. "And what criteria might that be?"

Something far enough from St. Louis that it was more than a causal drive away, but still in the south. A town with different cultural roots from his own to add interest. And a town small enough to allow him to forge new friendships and a new life quickly. "Someplace looking for a middle-grade math teacher, with moderate winters and an immediate opening." He adjusted the air conditioner. "The fact that my college roommate was from Alexandria helped this place catch my eye, as well."

"Oh, so you *do* have a connection to the area."

"Of sorts." Not that he intended to look Dave up. He planned to face forward, not back.

"Well, St. Louis's loss is our gain."

Graham searched for a new topic. They had an hour of road time ahead and he didn't want them to stray into any personal topics along the way. "Have you come up with a name for the choir yet?"

"Actually, I have."

"And that is?"

"Well, the first thing I thought of, naturally, was Joyful Noise. I mean, that name just pops to mind right off the bat, doesn't it?"

Which meant it probably wasn't the name she'd settled on. He didn't see her as one who'd go for the easy, obvious choice. But he was willing to play along. "Seems appropriate."

"Very. But I decided I'd prefer something with a touch more playfulness to it."

Of course she would. "Not one to take the easy road, are you?"

"Where's the fun in that?" Her grin made her look like a schoolgirl. "The next two I came up with were Noteworthy and Keynotes."

"Both good choices." Somehow he didn't think she'd selected one of those, either.

"Yes, but still not what I was looking for." She fiddled with her watch band. "I played with different word choices and came up with—" she cut her eyes at him as she paused dramatically and made a framing motion with her hands "—the Ding-a-lings." Her hands dropped in her lap. "What do you think?"

His lips twitched in spite of himself. "The Ding-a-lings? Well, if you're looking for something to put smiles on the faces of your audience I think you succeeded."

"I was striving for more of a we-don't-take-ourselves-too-seriously tone. Kind of wanting to focus on the fun and fellowship aspect as much as the ministry itself."

It said something about her that she was thinking through even these subtle aspects of her self-appointed ministry. "Sounds like you nailed it. I like it."

She relaxed. "I hope the others do, too. I had to put down a choir name when I registered us with the AGEHR and that's what I used." She swiped at the bangs on her forehead. "But it's easily changed if the group decides to go with something else."

Somehow he didn't think that would be the case. Her humor and enthusiasm were contagious. "My turn to ask a question. How did you come up with the idea of a handbell choir?"

Her brow puckered as she lifted a hand. Would she be able to talk if her hands were tied down?

"Like I told you when I first brought this up, I wanted something that would minister to the participants as much as the onlookers."

"Yes, I got that. And I can see this is a good fit for what you want to accomplish. But how did you stumble on this *particular* solution? I mean, a handbell choir's not something that would normally be on a person's radar screen unless she had experience with it or ties to someone who did."

"Oh. You mean sort of like my asking how you found Tippanyville? Well, when I first learned about the money and the stipulations tied to it, I wasn't really sure *what* I was going to do. It was all so overwhelming."

"I can imagine." What would he have done with such a responsibility?

She gave him a quick glance, and he remembered how inane those "I understand" comments had seemed after Annie died. It was impossible for anyone who hadn't gone through such a loss to really understand what it was like. She had no way of knowing he'd lost his wife, and he'd just as soon keep it that way.

But she merely nodded. "Anyway, I figured I'd take my time, look around the community and pray about it. I knew in my heart how Ray would have liked to be remembered and I was certain something would jump out as the obvious choice."

She punctuated her words with another of those expressive hand gestures. "But things are never quite that easy. And there's no such thing as a secret in a small town like Tippanyville. When word got out, suggestions poured in from all quarters. The high school athletic department where Ray coached talked to me about the need for new equipment lockers. The church I attend is renovating the fellowship hall and the committee mentioned some additional enhancements they could make with the extra money. The town council reminded me that they'd been trying for years to come up with funds to build a wider, sturdier footbridge in the park to replace the old one, and how Ray had been one of the project's staunchest supporters."

She took a deep breath before continuing. "There were lots of other suggestions along the same lines. All of them had merit, some were even quite worthy, and all of the proponents promised to be respectful of Ray's memory and to add some sort of prominent marker, dedicating their project to him."

Had it been him, he would probably have gone with one of those options. The footbridge seemed especially appropriate. There was a certain symbolic appeal to it. A reminder to those who saw it that Annie had lived a life worth remembering.

"But?" he prompted when she remained silent.

"But none of those ideas seemed quite right to me."

He kept silent, trying not to be judgmental. From where he sat the projects she mentioned seemed not only right but much more appropriate as a memorial to a loved one. They would definitely benefit more people in the community in the long run.

Not that he was in any position to judge the choice she'd made. Still, he had to wonder if she was trying to respect her husband's memory, or satisfy her own laudable desire to do something to help her friends.

Her hand fluttered then dropped back to her lap. "It's hard to explain, but I felt like none of those causes truly needed *this* money."

Not the response he'd expected. "What do you mean by 'this money'?"

She began ticking the items off on her fingers. "The high school has the PTA to help raise funds for things like new lockers—and believe me, they're good at it.

"The fellowship hall will serve its purposes just fine without any added monies—there's no ministerial value in gilding the lily.

"As for the footbridge, though the old one is small and showing some age, from a functional standpoint, it's all that's needed to get from one side of Bayou Cigale to the other. People have enjoyed the walking trails through the park for years just the way it is. If enough folks really want a fancy new stone bridge the city will find a way to make it happen."

She shook her head, seeming to shake off her momentary indecision in the process. "No, what I was looking for was a ministry that would reach out to people on an individual level and fill a need that no one else was likely to meet or even give much thought to." She nodded decisively. "That's what Ray would have wanted."

Then she gave a sheepish smile. "Listen to me rambling on and I didn't even answer your original question. You asked how I latched on to the handbell choir idea, didn't you? It was serendipitous really. Remember the Glory Be's?"

"Only what you told me the other afternoon. A quilting circle, wasn't it?"

"Quilting and *prayer* circle. Mother's been a member of the group since before I was born," she continued, "so I've known them all my life, sort of like a group of dear but eccentric aunts."

So prefixing their names with Miss was probably as much habit as courtesy.

"Anyway, they're always on the lookout for special needs in the community, so I asked them for suggestions. They're the ones who gave me Dana and Carrie's names. Of course, Joscelyn's need was already on my mind and heart."

She tucked the hair back from her face. "I still couldn't figure out just what I was going to do, though. Then I saw a special on television. They were running a feature on someone involved in a handbell choir. And interwoven in the discussion were clips of several choirs performing—one of them with wheelchair-bound members. And suddenly it all clicked. It was just the kind of thing that would help everyone on my list, and could benefit Desirée, too."

"Quite a chain of events to get you from there to here. As you say, serendipitous."

She nodded. "Serendipitous, yes. It was also an answered prayer."

There she went mentioning prayer again. Was it deliberate? And maybe she was right. Maybe God *had* answered her prayers. He'd seen it happen before. Just because He had turned a deaf ear to Graham didn't mean He ignored everyone's needs.

Graham caught her puzzled look and realized something of his thoughts must have been reflected in his face.

"What about your son?" he asked, grabbing for any change of subject. "Has Philip changed his mind about participating?"

"No, and I'm not pushing. Forcing him to participate wouldn't serve any useful purpose."

"True. So what's he going to do while you're holding practice sessions?"

"Work on his homework or sit around and watch, I guess. He's not old enough for me to feel comfortable leaving him on his own and I already lean on Mom more than I should."

"Have you thought about other ways to get him involved? Like helping with setup and being in charge of keeping things organized. You could even give him a roster and have him let you know when everyone's arrived."

He liked the approving smile she flashed his way.

"What a great idea. It'll sure beat having him just sitting around at loose ends while we practice." She twisted in her seat to face him fully. "You're going to make a great father someday."

Everything inside Graham contracted, closed off. He stared straight ahead, willing himself to breathe normally, to keep his expression blank. "You mentioned an end of October deadline for the group to prove itself," he managed to say. "Do you have anything specific in mind?"

She gave him a searching look, but after a moment accepted his change of subject. "Tippanyville has an annual Fall Festival at the end of October. It's like a minicarnival. There's a parade, craft and food booths, games for the kids—that sort of thing. Music is a big part of it, too. Several church choirs perform, as well as a number of local groups." She ticked items off on her fingers. "There's zydeco, jazz, high school bands—we even have an old-fashioned barbershop quartet. And this year, I plan to have a handbell choir under the pavilion, as well."

He had himself back under control now. More or less. "Sounds ambitious. We might want to talk with Mrs. Welborne about what sort of arrangements a new group like ours should attempt in the small amount of time we have."

"It's on my list."

Of course it was. He needed to find topics to keep her talking instead of asking questions. "So, you told me Joscelyn and Geralyn's stories. What about the other members? I assume they have similar stories since you went out of your way to recruit them."

She nodded. "Yes. And you're right—you need to know what their needs are so you can help minister to them."

Whoa—he'd signed up to help with the choir, not with her ministry.

But she'd already launched into her explanations. "Carrie Fontenot is recently widowed. She's not originally from around here so she doesn't have the local family support system that I had after Ray died. I'm hoping having something new to focus on and a reason to get out and mingle with people in new ways will help raise her spirits."

Is that what Reeny thought? That after losing someone you loved you could just raise your spirits by joining some social club? Didn't she remember what it had been like? Or was that all it had taken for her to cope and move on after her husband died?

"Dana Gleason is a high school senior," she continued, "and the granddaughter of the lady who's giving us the use of her building. I admit I don't know Dana very well. Wilma's son, Dana's father, moved to Dallas after he graduated from college and they only came back for special occasions. Anyway, Dana's folks died in a boating accident four months ago and she's been living with Wilma ever since. A loss like that is a lot for any seventeen-year-old to deal with. Add being abruptly uprooted from your big-city home and the friends you grew up with to land hundreds of miles away in a rural community like Tippanyville and you have the makings of a lonely, unhappy teen."

Graham frowned. "Was joining the group Dana's idea or her grandmother's?"

"Wilma told me she had to do some prodding. But Dana isn't being forced, if that's what you're worried about."

He foresaw trouble there. "Someone with those kinds of issues is going to need more than just warm fuzzies and group hugs. If she's not interested in being part of the choir you may have problems getting her to really commit."

She frowned. "Warm fuzzies and group hugs—is that what you think I'm trying to provide?"

He mentally winced. Seems he'd hurt her feelings. "My apologies. I wasn't trying to trivialize your efforts. But you know what I mean."

"I've found that, when you get a hurting person to look outside themselves and truly engage with others, it can go a long way toward helping them deal with their pain. That's going to be part of our job—to get her and the others engaged, to give them a sense of belonging."

Her intentions were commendable but from where he sat she was being overly optimistic. Things just weren't that simple.

As if she'd read his thoughts, she gave him a crooked

smile. "I'm not big-headed or foolish enough to think I can smooth over all of Dana's hurts, no more than I can with any of the others. But I can do my part to give her a place where she feels safe and welcome."

Okay, not so blindly Pollyannaish after all.

"And then there's Andrea Dufrene. Near the end of her senior year in high school, Andrea's mother was diagnosed with Parkinson's disease and Andrea became her main care-taker. While her friends were going off to college and getting married and starting families, Andrea was acting as nurse-companion to her mother. Mrs. Dufrene passed away six months ago, and Andrea, who is now twenty-eight, is finally free to do as she pleases. Only I think she believes the world passed her by."

Reeny was definitely taking on lost souls with her project. "And your two Glory Be's?"

"Miss Ada and Miss Clotile?" She grinned fondly. "They just volunteered because the Glory Be's wanted to show support. The sisters are two of the more musically minded of the group so they were a natural fit. But both have told me if there are others who want to join, or who I want to recruit, they'll step back and take on the role of standbys. They'll be a big help in making sure everyone feels welcomed and part of the group."

"Sort of like surrogate grandmothers, you mean."

Reeny laughed. It was a sound he was starting to enjoy.

"Don't let them hear you call them that," she said. "Oh, the stories I could tell you about the escapades those two have gotten into. Why, there was one time…"

Graham let her talk, enjoying the knack she had for telling stories in a way that made them come alive. He was begin-ning to see that her playful sense of humor, heart for others and determined optimism were all tightly intertwined to produce her infectiously heartwarming joie de vivre.

It was a very potent, hard-to-resist package.

Chapter Ten

Reeny exited the church building six hours later with a bounce to her step. This really could work! God had put just the right people in her life at just the right time. First Graham and now Edith.

"I think y'all are going to do just fine with that choir of yours." Edith Welborne stood with them on the church steps. "Graham, don't let the problems you had today get you down any. Playing handbells is different from playing the sort of instruments you're used to. Sometimes the really experienced musicians have the most trouble making the shift from playing an entire melody line to focus only on select notes. But you have a mighty talent and I could tell you're getting the hang of it already."

Graham gave a crooked smile. "Thanks, I think. And don't worry about me. I like a challenge."

"That's the spirit." She turned to Reeny. "As for you, girl, I've never seen anyone tackle the learning with such joy and determination."

Reeny gave the choir director a hug. "Thank you, Edith. I learned so much today."

Edith returned Reeny's hug, then gave Graham a handshake. "You two make a good team—you're going to do just fine. And you know you can pick up the phone and give me a call anytime you have questions."

Reeny stole a quick glance Graham's way, wondering what he thought of the "good team" comment. But his focus was on Edith.

"Thanks," he said. "I'll keep your number handy."

The choir director waved off his gratitude. "Happy to do it. Hope things work out for me to come up there next Saturday." She clasped her hands together. "I love the energy of a new group. It really fires up my enthusiasm for my own work."

Reeny nodded. "I'll call you tomorrow evening and let you know one way or the other."

With a final goodbye, Edith headed back inside and Graham hit the remote button to unlock his SUV.

Reeny hummed as she walked with him to the vehicle. Life was good. Not only had Edith given them lots of really great information on how to get things rolling with their group, but she'd allowed both of them to practice with the Enduring Faith choir.

Reeny had been more than a little intimidated at first, but the group had been so friendly and patient that before long she'd relaxed and started enjoying herself.

And Graham, even though he'd struggled at first, had hung in there and eventually hit his stride. She really admired his tenacity and ability to laugh at himself.

She slid into the SUV. "I think it went well today, but I'm feeling overwhelmed."

"It'll get easier." He turned the key in the ignition. "And, given what we learned today, I think your plan for the group to perform at the Fall Festival is doable. Assuming we get started right away."

"Everyone's going to be so excited to hear we're finally

ready to get started." She clicked her seat belt in place, feeling pleased with the world in general.

"Speaking of our meeting tomorrow, do you have a specific agenda in mind?"

Reeny hid a grimace. He made it sound so regimented. But she refused to let him spoil her mood. She could do agendas if that's what he wanted. "We can discuss what we learned today." She pulled out her notebook and pen. "And show off all the equipment that came in this week. Oh, and we also need to make sure everyone's available for the in-house clinic with Edith Saturday." Nothing to this agenda stuff. It was just another kind of list. And she could make sure the meeting itself was kept loose and informal. "Of course we also need to discuss the choir's name and decide on a practice schedule."

He nodded, apparently pleased with her list. "Sounds like a good plan. I assume you'll chair the meeting."

Did Graham plan things down to the nth degree all the time? "Actually, I figured we'd do it together. It'll help everyone get to know you better."

"I'll chime in when you need me to," he agreed. "But remember our deal. My role is only temporary, so best to start out as you mean to continue."

She mentally winced at this reminder of his eagerness to step down. She still hoped he'd decide to stay on permanently, but a deal was a deal. "Well, just don't be bashful about speaking up. You don't have to worry about stepping on my toes—I want to make sure we do this right."

"I'll keep that in mind. And don't worry," he added drily, "no one's ever had reason to accuse me of being bashful."

Reeny laughed. Good to know his sense of humor was still in there somewhere. "That I believe. So, can you think of anything else I need to put on the agenda for tomorrow?"

"I think you have it covered. I'll probably head over earlier in the day to work with the bells, now that I know a little about technique."

She liked the ring of enthusiasm in his voice. "And I'll go online tonight and check out the music suggestions Edith gave us. Maybe we can get together in the next day or so and make our picks."

He nodded. "Those chimes we heard today sounded pretty good. We might want to order a set at some point. Assuming the funds will stretch that far."

Reeny hid a satisfied smile. He'd said *we* not *you*. Maybe he was taking some ownership of the project after all. "I think we can cover it. Mrs. Plunkett was quite generous."

"Mrs. Plunkett—is she your benefactor?"

"Yes." Reeny paused, wondering how much she should say. It wasn't just that it was painful to talk about, she didn't really want to make him uncomfortable.

She glanced his way and suddenly realized she wanted to tell him the whole story. "I suppose I should fill you in on the details."

Graham mentally winced. He'd stepped right into something he'd been trying to avoid all day—personal confessions. "Sorry, I wasn't trying to pry."

"That's all right. It's not as if it's a secret. The rest of the town knows the story so you might as well hear it, too."

It didn't appear there was any stopping her now. And, glancing her way, he found he didn't really want to.

"I told you my husband died in a car accident three years ago. The rest of the story is that an elderly man named Harold Plunkett fell asleep at the wheel and his car drifted across the center line. Both he and Ray were killed in the subsequent crash."

Graham searched for something to say, but came up empty. His hand moved of its own accord, instinctively wanting to cover hers in a gesture of comfort. At the last moment he settled for a quick touch to her arm, then determinedly squeezed the steering wheel in a death grip, so his appendage wouldn't betray him again.

She flashed him a grateful smile, placing her own hand where his had been. The gesture sent a disorienting mix of warm satisfaction and alarm bells flashing through him. First that near embrace the other afternoon at the repurposed hat shop, and now this. He was as confused by his own behavior as by hers.

"I walked around in something of a fog those first few days, numb, not really able to absorb what had happened." She was no longer looking at him, but he noticed her hand still rested softly on the arm he'd touched. "Trying to hold everything together for the kids, knowing Ray was in a better place but still hurt and angry and scared."

Her words touched a familiar chord in him, stirred echoes of what he still felt.

"Thank goodness I had plenty of people looking out for me, supporting me, praying for me. I think it's the only thing that got me through those first few days."

The tenuous connection he'd felt withdrew. That was something he *didn't* identify with. The prayers and proffered comfort from his friends had sounded like well-meaning but hollow platitudes. How could they possibly have understood—they hadn't suffered *this* loss, *this* betrayal.

But she continued talking, unaware of his thoughts. "At the wake, a woman I'd never met came up to offer condolences to me and Ray's parents. She introduced herself as Ellen Plunkett, the widow of the other driver. Poor Lavinia, it was too much for her. She excused herself almost immediately."

Reeny paused a minute, but not before he heard the tiny hitch in her breathing. He'd been wrong that first day when he thought she didn't still feel a sense of loss.

"Mrs. Plunkett asked if we could sit and talk for a few minutes," she finally continued. "It didn't take long to see she felt a tremendous weight of guilt on her husband's behalf. She'd come all the way from Natchez to attend Ray's funeral, and that was on top of dealing with her own loss. We talked for a long time, mostly reminiscing about our husbands. When she left, she asked for my mailing address."

How could she have faced the woman and not felt some bitterness?

"Mrs. Plunkett wrote to me several times after that and I always responded. Then three months ago her lawyer contacted me. She'd passed away and named me in her will. It seemed she'd never touched the money from her husband's life insurance policy. That's where the memorial fund came from. And she left it up to me to decide what form the memorial should take."

She turned to him with another of those fluttery hand gestures. "So, there you have it. The chain of events that brought us to where we are today."

"Quite a story." And quite different from his own. The old litany of injuries played out in his mind again. She hadn't faced weeks of uncertainty. She hadn't had to make the hard choices he had. She hadn't put misguided trust in God to answer prayers for a good outcome.

But a small part of him wondered if she would have made it through that situation better than he had.

He caught a faint whiff of the vanilla scent she wore, a perfect fit for the warm, down-to-earth person she was, and he realized his mantle of bitterness didn't sit quite as comfortably on his shoulders as it had before.

Chapter Eleven

Graham shook hands with the petite blonde who'd introduced herself as Geralyn Vedros. Noting she'd entered the shop with a slight limp, he'd already figured out this was the former dancer Reeny had told him about.

She gave him a teasing smile. "So you're the brave soul who Reeny convinced to help whip us into shape."

He returned her smile. "Guilty. But Reeny's the director— I'm only here to lend a hand."

She patted his arm. "Ah, but without you she wouldn't have agreed to lead, so we have you to thank. Besides, I don't think she'll let you sit on the sidelines much." With a wave, she moved on to mingle with the others present.

A few minutes later, Reeny moved to the center of the room. "Okay, I think everybody's here." Without raising her voice, she had everyone's attention. She would have been a natural as a schoolteacher.

"Why don't y'all grab your refreshments and take a seat," she continued. "I hope everyone's had a chance to meet the newest member of our group, Graham Lockwood. Graham has very generously agreed to step up and serve as assistant choir director."

Before he could so much as raise a brow, she immediately qualified her statement. "At least for the time being."

He accepted the smattering of applause with a short bow.

"The two of us went down to Lafayette yesterday to meet with Edith Welborne," she continued. "Edith is the director of the Enduring Faith Handbell Choir there, and she gave us lots of great advice on how to get the ball rolling. We're going to share some of that with y'all this afternoon."

Reeny fiddled with the locket she wore around her neck. "First, though, I want to say again how much I appreciate the way all of y'all have helped bring this project to life. Ray would've loved seeing this come together." Her smile included everyone. "It's going to take a lot of commitment from each of you as we move forward." After a short pause, she flashed an infectious grin. "But that doesn't mean we can't have fun along the way."

That earned her smiles and a few laughs. Graham studied their faces, seeing subtle signs of support, pride and enthusiasm. Did Reeny understand the gift she had for making people feel comfortable and valued?

"Okay, then," she said, "before we move on to serious business, let's talk about coming up with a name for the group."

"Seeing as how the money was designated specifically to honor Ray," Joscelyn said, "I figure we'd go with the Ray Landry Memorial Handbell Choir."

"I appreciate the thought, but I think that's too big a mouthful. And those of you who knew Ray would know he'd think it was pretentious."

"Maybe the Tippanyville Community Handbell Choir?" Ada offered.

"That's simpler, but I was thinking we might want to go with something a bit more unexpected and fun."

"Joyful Noise seems fitting." That suggestion came from Geralyn.

Graham caught the what-did-I-tell-you look she cut his way.

"Quite appropriate," she said. "But I did some looking online and there are already a bunch of choirs with that name or a variation of it. I was hoping we could come up with something a bit more unique."

"Too bad Glory Be is already taken," Carrie offered. "How about something simple like the Tippanyville Ringers?"

Ada gave her sister a censoring sniff. "The girl says she's looking for something with pizzazz to it."

Graham cleared his throat. "I think Reeny has one she'd like to suggest." He ignored the I-wasn't-ready-for-that look she flashed his way.

Joscelyn shot her an exasperated look. "Well, why didn't you say so? Out with it, *chère*."

Reeny waggled the pen she was holding between her fingers. "Okay, but keep in mind we're just throwing out ideas. We want something we'll all be happy with." She paused a moment, then grinned. "I'm thinking The Ding-a-lings has a nice ring to it. Pun intended."

There were a few surprised blinks and then some murmuring as folks thought it over. Finally, Clotile spoke up, amusement deepening her already thick Cajun accent. "Oh me, I like it. The Ding-a-lings. Makes me smile when I say it."

Ada nodded. "Me too. But let's add Tippanyville to it."

"I think we have our name," Joscelyn said. "The Tippanyville Ding-a-lings."

Reeny looked around the room. "Everybody okay with that or should we throw out a few more ideas?"

As Graham had expected, everyone was happy with the name she'd suggested.

She glanced his way. "Why don't you talk about schedules next?" They'd agreed earlier that he would lead this part of the discussion.

He nodded and moved to take her place at the center of the room. "One of the most important factors in any choir's success is the commitment of its members. That's especially true for a handbell choir. A handbell choir isn't like a vocal choir or another large orchestra. If someone is missing it's like missing keys on a piano keyboard—you can't cover it up easily and it throws everything off. And it's next to impossible to find a last-minute replacement."

Graham scanned the room, taking time to meet each of their gazes. "So if you don't think you can attend the practice sessions week in and week out, speak up now or see Reeny or myself after the meeting. I give you my word—no one will think less of you for bowing out at this point."

"Don't you worry," Joscelyn said, "we'll be here."

Agreements echoed across the room.

"All right then, let's talk about what days and times will work best for everyone. Mrs. Welborne suggested two sessions a week of about an hour each for the first month or so, and then, if we're making good progress, we could probably make do with a single one-and-a-half hour session each week."

After a great deal of discussion, Graham brought the group back to order. "It sounds like Mondays and Thursdays at six in the evening will work best for the majority. Is there anyone who just can't live with that?"

No one spoke up. "Then it appears we have our practice schedule." With a sweep of his hand, he turned the meeting back over to Reeny.

"Now, I know this is kind of short notice," she said, "but Edith is willing to spend the better part of the day with us next Saturday. She can help us figure out ringing positions, demonstrate techniques, help us select the right music so we get started on the right foot—that sort of thing. It'll mean committing five hours of your weekend, but Edith is giving us even more. So, how many of you are available?"

Every hand in the room went up.

"Wonderful. We'll hold off on practice sessions until after the clinic, then start up the following Monday."

She moved to the counter and picked up a DVD, which was his signal to roll the television to the middle of the room. "We have a short video that provides some general information about handbells and demonstrates simple ringing techniques. We'll play it and answer any questions you have as well as we can. Graham and I can demonstrate some of what we learned yesterday and then those of you who want to can try the bells for yourselves. We'll stay as long as you like."

They played through the instructional DVD twice, then Graham moved to the back of the room where the handbells were set out. Several of the members drifted over to join him, but no one seemed willing to be the first to handle a bell.

Not an auspicious beginning.

Finally Graham pointed to Desirée. "Why don't you come up here and show all these grownups how easy this is."

As he'd expected, the eight-year-old stepped forward and eagerly took the bell Graham handed her. He worked with her for several minutes, demonstrating the proper way to hold the bell, then walked through the downward, outward, upward, backward motion of ringing, ending with damping the bell against his shoulder. After a couple of tries, she was able to move her hand in something approaching the proper motion.

After congratulating the little girl on her success, Joscelyn stepped forward and lifted one of the larger bells. "Okay, Mr. Assistant Director, why don't you show me how it's done one more time."

Reeny hummed softly as she and Desirée gathered up the paper plates and washed the coffeemaker. It had been a great first meeting for the choir. And to top that off, she'd noticed how closely Philip paid attention to what was going on. Maybe he'd eventually want to do more than just watch. The fact that Graham was so hands-on certainly helped.

She glanced across the room where the two males were folding up the last of the chairs. Graham was providing a great example for her son. Her brother Jake didn't get a chance to come around as much as he used to and Philip could use some male influence in his life.

Graham glanced her way just then and she quickly busied herself with tying up the trash bag, grateful he couldn't read her thoughts.

Once everything was put away, Reeny turned to Philip. "Help your sister carry this stuff out to the car while I speak to Mr. Lockwood for a minute."

"Yes, ma'am. Come on, Desi."

As the door closed behind the kids, her traitorous mind pulled up an image of the last time they'd been here. Feeling suddenly self-conscious, she blurted out her question. "So, how do you think it went?"

He gave her a questioning glance, no doubt taking note of her rattled tone. "It was a good start-up meeting. They're an eclectic group, though. Their music experience and aptitude appears to be all over the place, as is their enthusiasm level. Do you think they'll be able to pull together as a group?"

Forgetting her momentary embarrassment, she tilted up her chin. "They will, if we do our job right."

"Look, I'm not being critical, just trying to be objective. Yes, Joscelyn shows real promise. And Ada, Clotile, Desirée and Andrea are all enthusiastic, though their aptitude has yet to be tested."

He stared straight at her, his expression daring her to disagree. "As for Dana, Geralyn and Carrie, the jury's still out on them. And don't forget you're three members short of the optimal choir size."

"It's only the first meeting. Just have a bit of faith." She touched his arm and then withdrew when she felt his reaction. Had he flinched at her touch or her mention of faith?

His expression didn't give anything away. "Oh, I'm not planning to jump ship if that's what you're worried about." He spoke as if nothing had happened. "I just wanted to warn you not to build your hopes up too high."

He indicated she was to precede him out the door, and she snatched her purse and complied. He waited long enough for her to lock the door, then with a wave, climbed into his SUV.

As Reeny loaded her kids into her car, she gave a mental sigh. It didn't seem as if she'd ever figure the man out.

But one thing she did know, she was very glad he wasn't planning to jump ship.

The next morning Graham slowed to a walk as he approached the water fountain conveniently located along the park's walking trail. From as far back as he could remember he'd loved to run. He'd been on his high school track team and been pretty good at it. His schedule hadn't allowed him to join the team in college, but he made time to run two or three times a week even then. Once he'd started teaching, he found running not only helped him keep in shape but helped clear his mind and prepare him for the day ahead.

Then, in those dark days after Annie died, running had become more than an exercise. It had kept him sane whenever the nightmare his life had become threatened to overwhelm him. He'd pounded the pavement relentlessly, running until he could barely put one foot in front of the other, day in and day out, for months.

Eventually he'd settled into a more normal routine. He still ran every day, and even if it meant getting up a couple of hours early on school days, it was worth it.

Graham took a big swig of the tepid fountain water, then

started into his cool-down routine. He liked this part of the day, the feeling that he was watching the town wake up, stretch its arms and come to life.

A pickup lumbered by, headed toward the main highway. The streetlights winked out and he heard a bird trill from a nearby tree. The sound put him in mind of the handbells, which put him in mind of Reeny. Not that she'd been much out of his thoughts lately. He'd been in Tippanyville just under two weeks and already the woman had turned his life upside down. The thing was, he still hadn't decided if that was a good thing or a bad thing.

A second early-morning jogger took a turn at the water fountain, giving Graham something to focus on besides his jumbled thoughts.

He'd noticed this runner at the park before, a younger man with an athlete's build. This morning, rather than continuing on his way, the young man stuck out a hand. "Hi, there. I'm Jeff Broussard."

Graham paused from his cool-down and took his hand, giving it a firm shake. "Graham Lockwood. Glad to meet you."

"I've seen you out here before. You set a punishing pace."

"You're no slacker yourself."

"Thanks. Comes from years of involuntary practice." The young man grinned wryly. "I had the chance to run lots of laps in high school."

"Tough gym teacher?"

"Football coach. And yeah, Coach was tough on all of us. But always fair." Jeff drew his shoulders back and turned his head from side to side. "You're the new math teacher over at the elementary school, aren't you?"

"That's me. And you?"

"I'm a fireman."

Graham raised a brow. "And you spend your spare time running?"

Jeff laughed. "Tippanyville is not like the big metropolitan areas. We normally have long periods—and I'm talking weeks—between call outs. Which is a good thing, I know. But it means I spend a lot of time sitting around the station with not a lot to do. Running helps keep me in shape."

"I guess I never thought of it that way." Graham straightened. "Well, it was good to meet you, but I need to head back and take my shower or I'll be *getting* tardy slips instead of handing them out."

"Actually, if you got just another minute, there's something I wanted to ask you."

Graham paused, noting the uncertainty in the young man's voice. "Oh?"

"You're the one helping Mrs. Landry organize that handbell choir of hers, aren't you?"

"Guilty as charged." Graham kept his tone light but watched Jeff warily. He remembered Reeny mentioning that not everyone in town was happy with her choice of how to spend the money. Did the fireman want to recruit him to help point her in another direction?

Jeff rubbed his neck, looking slightly embarrassed. "Well, I don't know that I'd be very good at it, but if you'll have me, I'd like to join up with you folks."

The unexpected response threw Graham off for a minute. "It's really Mrs. Landry's call, but I'm sure she'd be happy to have you." And then some. Finally, a male recruit. "Mind if I ask why?"

"I heard she was looking for a few more folks to fill out the roster. And Coach, that is, Mr. Landry, well, he helped me through some pretty rough times, and I figure helping her out is the closest I'm gonna be able to get to paying him back. Besides, this choir is all about doing something to honor his memory, isn't it?"

"That's what I've been told."

"Well then, that settles it." The young fireman straightened his shoulders. "Definitely count me in. And I'll just bet I can get one or two other guys from the station to join up too if she needs more members."

"I'm sure Mrs. Landry will appreciate the sentiment." He smiled. "But don't go doing any arm twisting. We only want members who really *want* to be there."

"Understood. But like I said, I'd do anything to help out Coach or his family."

Jeff's sincerity was obvious. Ray Landry must have been quite a man if he could still elicit this kind of loyalty three years after he was gone.

"We haven't had any real practice sessions yet so you won't have to worry about playing catch-up. There's an all-day clinic scheduled for Saturday at ten. Think you can make it?"

"I'll be there."

"You know where we meet?" At Jeff's nod, he waved. "I really *do* need to go now. See you Saturday."

Graham headed toward his vehicle, looking forward to giving Reeny the good news.

Reeny gave Desirée one last push on the swing then stepped back. "You're on your own now, t-girl. Momma's tired."

Glancing over the azalea hedge, she spied Graham wheeling a lawn mower out of his storage shed.

"Hey, neighbor," she said as she strolled closer. "Getting in some yard work?"

He left the mower and joined her at the hedge. "Yep. I figure I ought to try to trim this back before it requires a bush hog."

He really did have a nice smile. If only he'd use it more often.

"By the way," he continued, "I bumped into Jeff Broussard at the park this morning. You know him?"

"Jeff? Sure. He's a good guy. Had a rough adolescence, but he's straightened himself out and has turned into a really stand-up guy—holding down a job as a fireman, taking online classes to get his business degree and caring for a younger brother."

Hard to think of Jeff as an adult. She still remembered him as one of the high school football players Ray had taken under his wing. Her husband had had a positive influence on so many boys who needed guidance over the years.

She pulled her thoughts back to Graham. "What about him?"

"He asked about joining the choir."

She was taken aback, then gave him a suspicious frown. "Did you do any arm twisting? I know I said I'd like to recruit some guys but—"

He held both hands up, palm out. "Whoa. Jeff approached me out of the blue. Before he introduced himself the only thing I knew about him was that he was the other fool who got up at the crack of dawn to jog in the park."

She relaxed. "In that case, I hope you said yes."

"Told him I'd run it by you, but as far as I was concerned he was in."

"Did he say why he wanted to join?"

"Something about owing it to your husband." He tilted his head to one side. "I thought you'd be happy about it."

"Oh, I am. It's just unexpected is all." Then she laughed. "Listen to me. I ask God to help me out and when He does I go and act all surprised."

She saw that flicker that always crossed his expression whenever she talked of God or prayer. But she refused to change her way of talking just to make him more comfortable. "Not only will Jeff make a great addition to the choir,

I couldn't have found a better role model for Philip if I'd tried. With such a macho figure ringing bells, there's no way Philip can keep thinking of it as a sissy undertaking."

Oops, that didn't come out quite right. "That's not to say you aren't a good example, as well. It's just—"

"I know, I know. I don't count because I'm not really part of the choir itself."

"Exactly." She brushed at a fly. "That brings us up to nine members. If Philip decides to join, that'll be ten. So we just need one more to have a full slate."

"Jeff did mention he might be able to convince a friend or two to join him. So keep your fingers crossed."

"I'll do better than that. I'll pray about it."

This time he didn't flinch. Instead he looked at her straight on. "It's been my experience that one works as well as the other."

And with that shocking statement, he turned and went back to his mower.

Chapter Twelve

Reeny set the bells down. "You're very patient, Edith. I just hope I'm as good a student as you are a teacher."

Edith had been working with her and Graham for almost an hour, giving them an overview of the techniques she would be using with the group today and giving them pointers on what sort of things to look for from a director's perspective. Reeny's head was swimming with information.

"I have every confidence that you two will do fine. I'm already impressed with the equipment and facilities you have here. It's unusual to find a secular beginner level group that is so well equipped and has a dedicated practice facility like this one."

"We've been blessed all right." Reeny glanced at her watch. "The members should start arriving soon."

Edith nodded. "Well, I think we're ready. Just one more thing. Even if this is going to be a fun and fellowship kind of group, you still need to set a few ground rules going in so everyone understands what's expected of them. I'll help with the technical aspects, but the rest should come from you."

Reeny nodded and grabbed her notebook. "I understand about it needing to come from us. But can you help me out on the expectations part? I mean, what kinds of things should we think about?"

"It's mostly commonsense stuff. Things like attendance and tardiness issues, care and handling of bells and other equipment, mutual respect among members—especially patience with those who struggle a bit more with the learning process. Also, you want to encourage your ringers not to be afraid to make mistakes. Timidity, the fear of looking foolish or inept, can be as much a hindrance as lack of skill."

Reeny jotted the last of her notes. "I think we can handle that."

"Keep that in mind as you observe how things go today and then come up with your guidelines to present at the first regular practice session." Edith glanced at Graham. "With your choir director experience, you should have an idea of what I'm talking about."

The bell jingled as the outer door opened. Joscelyn stepped inside, followed by Desirée and Philip. Reeny had dropped the kids off at her mother's earlier and asked Joscelyn to pick them up on her way over.

"Hello." Joscelyn waggled her fingers their way. "Y'all just keep doing whatever you were doing. The kids and I plan to check out the goodies over on the counter."

"Help yourselves," Reeny answered. "We were just finishing up." She turned back to Edith. "If you want to take a break while we're waiting for the rest of the crew, there's soft drinks and water in the refrigerator as well as some fresh fruit. And that plate on the counter has some oatmeal cookies."

Jeff was the next one through the door, and he had his younger brother in tow.

"Mrs. Landry, if it's okay with you, Mark here would like to join the handbell group, too."

Reeny eyed the high school senior with skepticism. "It's perfectly okay with me, as long as you didn't twist his arm."

Mark gave her a boyish smile. "No, ma'am, it was my idea. I figure this is the sort of thing that'll look good on my college applications. I need all the help I can get."

"Don't let him fool you." Jeff's pride in his brother was obvious. "With his grades, Mark'll be able to get into most any college he wants to."

Mark elbowed his brother. "I'm good, but don't lay it on too thick, bro."

Their interaction reminded Reeny of the way she and Jake had acted when she was Mark's age. She still thought he was pretty special. "Well in that case, welcome to the Tippanyville Ding-a-lings. We'll get started as soon as everyone else gets here."

"Yes, ma'am." The two wandered over to check out the bells.

Graham handed her a cookie. "I see Jeff brought a friend along. New recruit?"

"Uh-huh. His brother, Mark."

"So, you now have not one but two male members to round out the group, just like you wanted."

"And *they* sought *me* out without my lifting a finger. Isn't God good?"

Graham wondered if Reeny was deliberately trying to provoke him with her constant references to God and prayer. Or was that her normal way of speaking? Whatever the case, he'd decided not to let it get under his skin. He'd just think of it as an automatic response—the way one said "God bless you" after a sneeze.

A few minutes later he spied Philip sitting alone at the counter and strolled over to join him. He'd been watching the way the boy reacted to Jeff and Mark's presence. When Reeny's son had first realized the two Broussards were not only volunteering to join, but actually seemed enthusiastic about the whole thing, his eyes had gotten wide with surprise and then he'd grown thoughtful.

"You know," Graham said as he grabbed a cookie from the plate, "according to Mrs. Welborne, this choir would really perform better with eleven members rather than ten."

"Oh?"

"Yep. And your sister's a lot younger than the other members. She'd probably feel better having someone closer to her age to practice with, don't you think?"

Philip shrugged. "I suppose."

"I was just wondering, do you think you could see your way to filling in, at least until we can find an eleventh member?"

Philip tried to look nonchalant. "I guess. I mean, if you really need someone to fill in. Just for now, though."

"Understood. Why don't you let your mom know."

Philip hopped off his stool and sauntered over to Reeny.

Graham nodded in satisfaction as he watched Reeny's face light up. When she glanced his way with a silent "Thank you" lighting her eyes, he found himself standing a bit taller.

Reeny didn't have time to give Graham a proper thank-you. Carrie was the last to arrive, and as soon as she was introduced to Edith, it was time to call everyone to order. After announcing and welcoming the three new members, she turned the floor over to Edith.

"All right everyone," Edith began, "today we're going to be working hard and learning lots of new things. But I promise you, we're also going to have fun while we do it."

Reeny and Graham took their places behind the other members where they could observe and assist. She felt a bit nervous. Then she glanced over at Graham who surprised her with a quick thumbs-up and wink for her eyes alone. It put a grin on her face and gave her a boost of much-needed confidence.

"For those of you who don't yet know how to read music," Edith was saying, "don't let that worry you. I'm going to show you some tricks that'll have you ringing right on cue, just like the pros. But for now, we're just going to focus on technique—how to hold the bell, the proper way to ring it and how to damp it…."

The next couple of hours passed quickly. Edith was very patient, going over the exercises and techniques slowly and repeatedly. Reeny and Graham handled the one-on-one work with those who got behind or needed a little extra attention. Before long, Reeny found that she and Graham were able to communicate with just a glance or nod. Edith was right, the two of them did make a good team.

All morning long, the memory of not only that wink but of the hand he'd played in nudging Philip into joining the choir kept a smile on her face. Really, the man could be quite charming, in a gruff, reserved kind of way.

"I can't tell you how much we appreciate your coming in today, Edith." Reeny had walked the choir director to her car. "This has been so helpful. I think everyone got a lot out of it."

"You've got a good group here. They seem enthusiastic and that's half the battle. You're going to do just fine. And I expect an invite to your first performance."

"It's a deal."

Once Edith was gone, Reeny joined Graham and the kids inside to help straighten up.

They were just about done, when Reeny's mom walked in.

Surprised by the visit, Reeny paused in the act of folding a chair closed. "Hi, Mom. What's up?"

"I just thought I'd drop by and see if anyone was interested in a slice of the peanut butter pie I whipped up this morning. I have some vanilla ice cream to go with it," she added, as if extra incentive might be required.

"I am!" Philip turned pleading eyes Reeny's way. "Can we, Mom? Please?"

Desirée's expression and quickly signed "please" was no less entreating. Her mother's peanut butter pie was a family favorite. Which would put Reeny firmly in the camp of the Grinch if she said no.

"All right and thanks. But we can't stay long."

"Graham, I'd be pleased if you would join us, as well."

"Thank you, ma'am, but that's not really necessary. I—"

"You don't like peanut butter pie?"

"It's not that. I'm certain it's delicious. I just don't want to intr—"

"Then I insist you join us." Reeny's mom lifted her chin. "Besides, I have an ulterior motive for my invitation. I wanted to talk to you and Reeny about the choir."

Reeny tilted her head, more than a little suspicious of what that ulterior motive might be. Nevertheless, she gave Graham a warning look. "You might as well give in. Mom can be quite persuasive when she has her mind set on something."

"Sort of like her daughter?" he asked drily.

Not the least bit insulted, Reeny responded with a firm nod. "Exactly."

Looking very pleased with herself, Reeny's mom took each grandchild by the hand. "That's settled then. I'll just take Philip and Desirée with me while you two finish up here. Reeny, you can give Graham directions."

She paused at the door and turned back around. "And take however much time you need. I know you might want to review how things went today and set plans for the next session. The kids and I will be fine."

Graham wondered what that was all about. What could Reeny's mother possibly want to discuss with him?

"Thank you."

He turned, surprised by her words. "For what?"

"For giving Philip the nudge to join the group in a manner that made him feel he was helping out. I don't know what you said to him, but it worked."

"You're welcome." Uncomfortable with her thanks, he changed the subject. "So, what's your take on how things went today?"

"Quite well. What about you?"

He had mixed feelings. "Honest opinion? The good news is you have the numbers now. And I think some of them have enough talent and enthusiasm to be really good."

"And the bad news?"

No point in soft-pedaling this. "It's obvious Dana is only here because her grandmother is insisting. She doesn't seem to take any joy in what she's doing. And Carrie seems just plain lost and afraid to touch anything."

Reeny didn't seem overly worried about his concerns. "Give them time. This was just the first session. Dana's been through a lot in a short period of time, and I think she's afraid to get too invested in anything right now. Besides, I believe the Good Lord was watching out for her when he sent Mark our way. Having someone her age in the group will be good for her, you'll see."

Did the woman see God's hand in *everything?*

"As for Carrie," she continued, "I think she really does want to be a part of this. Otherwise, why would she even bother to come? If she seems lost it's because we haven't done a good enough job of pulling her in yet."

He shook his head, unconvinced. "I know you want to help these folks, but we can't be all things to all people. I just want you to prepare yourself for the fact that you may lose one or both of them before the festival."

She nodded and dropped the subject. They made good use

of the rest of the time Mrs. Perette had given them, discussing the ground rules they wanted to set and strategizing on how to divide the duties for their next practice session.

Despite her bent toward misguided optimism, Reeny had a practical head on her shoulders. It surprised him just how complementary their ideas and leadership styles were.

Unfortunately, discussing choir business with her only partially succeeded in getting his wayward mind off areas his more logical side wanted no part of—like how he'd like to have another excuse to hold her. What in the world was wrong with him?

At last they called it quits and headed for Mrs. Perette's house. Graham followed Reeny, parking in front of a well-shaded, yellow-and-white residence.

As he followed Reeny up a couple of shallow steps to the spacious wraparound porch, he realized this was very likely the home she'd grown up in. He got the quick impression of homey comfort—a slatted porch swing lined with pillows, a wooden rocker, a couple of roomy wicker chairs, plants in hanging baskets—before they reached the front door.

The front door itself looked like a piece of folk art. He'd glimpsed several of the screen doors around town adorned with one sort of decorative metal cutout or another, but this was the first one he'd seen close-up. A large heron stood in a grouping of cattails, austerely staring at something to their left.

Reeny gave the bird a quick touch before she reached for the door.

"Old friend?" he asked with a nod toward the figure.

She grinned. "Henry here used to watch over me when I'd sit on the porch playing with jacks, or dolls or just reading a book."

Graham had a sudden image of her as a little girl doing those things and smiled in spite of himself.

Reeny knocked and then walked in with a "We're here" hail.

"I'm back in the kitchen."

Graham noticed the proliferation of photographs on the walls as they passed through the living room. He found himself wishing he had the time to study them closer.

"Come on in. The kids are out in the backyard." Mrs. Perette set a couple of generous slices of pie on the kitchen table. "Do you like yours topped with whipped cream or vanilla ice cream?"

Graham smiled. "I'm a vanilla ice cream fan myself."

"I'll have mine plain, thanks." Reeny fetched the spoons while her mom retrieved the ice cream.

To Graham's relief, after Reeny took her first bite, she was ready to get down to business. "So, what did you want to discuss with us?"

"Well, I'm not interested in joining, so you can set your mind at ease on that point. But I would like to attend your practice sessions."

That was it? Graham wasn't certain what he'd expected, but this seemed rather anticlimactic.

From the expression on Reeny's face, she felt the same. "Mom, you know you're more than welcome to drop by any time. But why?"

"To support you of course. And I don't want to just drop by. I can be audience, cheerleader, mascot—whatever. I can make sure the refreshments are set up, and clean-up is taken care of and—"

Reeny placed a hand over her mom's. "Stop. You don't need to do all of that."

"Well, it won't be any trouble. For the most part I figure I'll crochet and watch y'all practice. Which I'm sure I'll enjoy. But what I really have to offer you comes after the session."

Graham leaned back. Ah, so there was more.

There was a suspicious light in Reeny's eyes. "And what might that be?"

"Me, I remember back when you were younger I helped Francine Nicholls coach the girl's little league softball team. We had to carve out time away from the team so we could discuss how things were going, the individual players' strengths and weaknesses and plan our strategies. I imagine for you two it's going to be the same. And since Philip and Desirée are part of the choir, it's going to be hard for y'all to find that time. So, I can take my *petit-enfants* back here with me after each practice session and give y'all fifteen or twenty minutes to discuss whatever you need to while you're closing shop. And then Reeny, you can pick them up on your way home." She sat back. "What do you say?"

"Mom, that's very generous of you but—"

"No, I *want* to do this. Besides, it'll give me a chance to be part of this thing you are doing."

Reeny turned to Graham. "What do you think?"

What he thought was that Reeny had learned how to be persuasive—and selfless—right here at home.

Chapter Thirteen

Reeny watched the choir members mingle and chat while they waited for the last few people to arrive. She was nervous, no getting around that. How in the world was she going to direct the group when she didn't know what she was doing herself? Everything Edith had taught her about directing seemed to suddenly fly out of her head.

Graham would be so much better at this. If he wasn't so stubborn—

She stopped that line of thought cold. They had an agreement and she planned to live up to her end. She should be grateful for all the many things he'd done already. Just this afternoon he'd helped her work up a simple set of ground rules for the group.

Besides, she'd already had this conversation with God.

Heavenly Father, help me remember this is not about me. Help me focus instead on the needs of those around me.

Andrea arrived just then, carrying what appeared to be a large wooden sign. It had a rounded top, was flat on the sides and bottom and was stained a light oak color.

Both Graham and Jeff stepped forward to help her.

Reeny joined them as they placed it on the counter.

"I worked on this over the weekend." Andrea sounded nervous, as if she wasn't certain how her work would be viewed. "I thought our building ought to have a more appropriate sign than the one currently hanging over the door."

Reeny studied the woodwork, tracing the curved contours with a finger. The carving was beautifully done. The name of the choir was deeply etched in playful lettering. A groove outlined the inner contours. And beneath the name she'd etched a pair of crossed handbells.

"This is absolutely beautiful." Reeny gave the artist a quick hug. "Thank you so much for doing this."

The group had all crowded around to get a better look and there were a number of enthusiastic agreements.

Andrea blushed. "Thank you. I brought some permanent markers in different colors. I thought we could all sign it on the back before we hung it up."

"What a wonderful idea."

Andrea handed Graham and Reeny each a marker. "You two go first."

Reeny signed her name on one end with a flourish and Graham took the opposite end. His handwriting was firm and even, very much reflective of the man himself. Once he'd finished signing he lifted Desirée up so she could sign next.

There was some good-natured haggling over marker colors and the staking out of prime spots for signatures as the rest of the members took their turns.

After Jeff signed his name he turned to Reeny. "We'll need a ladder to hang this. I'll throw one in the back of my truck and bring it with me Thursday."

Before she could say more than "Thank you," Mark caught her attention. "You know, this gives me an idea. Dana and I are in Mr. Malvern's senior art class. He's told us we have to turn in a finished project by midsemester. He set some criteria on medium and composition, but the subject is up to us." He turned to Dana. "What do you think about doing companion pieces to hang up in here?"

Dana looked first startled, then shyly pleased that Mark had singled her out. "I'd like that."

"Great! Maybe we can brainstorm ideas after school tomorrow."

"Well, I don't intend to let *les jeunes* have all the fun," Miss Ada declared. "I think I might just find me some bright fabric and make curtains for the window."

Reeny's heart warmed. Bless Andrea—her gesture had gone a long way to getting the group off on the right foot. This family feeling was just what she'd hoped would happen, only she hadn't expected to see it this soon.

She caught Graham watching her. He gave a subtle thumbs-up signal, letting her know he'd read her thoughts.

Feeling a renewed sense of purpose, Reeny took a deep breath, smiled and moved to the center of the room. "Okay everyone, let's go ahead and get started."

Once she had everyone's attention, she dove right into the items on her list. "Before we begin the exercises, there's a few announcements to make. First off, since next Monday is Labor Day I'd like to move that session to Tuesday. Is everyone okay with that?"

When no one objected, she pointed to the poster she and Graham had hung earlier. "Next up, Graham and I want to discuss a set of guidelines we developed…."

Reeny was amazed by how quickly the hour flew by. Before she knew it she was watching her mom escort the kids out of the building and calling out to her not to spoil the kids' supper.

When she turned back around, Graham was folding and putting away the chairs. She watched him from the corner of her eye as she moved to the coffeemaker. As he carried the last load across the room she saw the play of muscles along his arms. No one could honestly accuse him of being a flabby desk jockey.

She gave herself a mental shake. Better to think about his other admirable qualities. Like how well his teaching skills carried over into these sessions. He was good at this, no doubt about it—patient and encouraging with those who needed a little extra help, firm with those who needed the extra push. Made her glad Philip was in his math class.

Graham turned around just then, dusting his hands. Had he caught her staring?

"Dana has definitely perked up since the last session," she said quickly.

"I agree." He gave a concessional bow. "And I will admit you pegged it right when you said Mark's presence would make a difference. I heard them talking as they left—they seem pretty excited about that art project."

"And Carrie will come around, too. She just needs a little more time."

"We'll see."

Reeny decided to let his comment pass. "I think maybe by next practice we'll be ready to move on from these exercise pieces." She tucked the hair at her temple back behind her ears. "I located a site on the Web that has recordings of handbell music. Most of the pieces Edith recommended are posted there. Maybe you could come over to the house this evening and we could listen to them and decide which ones to select."

He hesitated and Reeny wondered if she was pushing too hard again. Did he think she was being forward?

But he finally nodded. "Sounds good." Then he smiled. "Since you fed me last time, why don't I pick up a couple of pizzas and bring them over so you don't have to worry with supper?"

"You're on." Reeny tried not to read too much into the offer. After all, he was probably just being polite, à la his grandmother's teachings.

But a part of her couldn't help but hope he enjoyed her company—and the kids', too, of course—enough to want to spend a little extra time with them.

Graham pushed back from the table in Reeny's dining room satisfied that the pizza had been a hit. Between him and the three Landrys, the two pizzas had disappeared in nothing flat.

"All right, kids," Reeny said as she stood, "you two have kitchen duty tonight while Mr. Lockwood and I take care of some handbell choir business. Philip, when y'all get done in here, would you quiz Desirée on her spelling words one more time, please?"

She turned to Graham. "My computer is just down the hall in my office."

So, he'd get to see where she worked. Should be interesting.

The first thing he noticed, before he ever entered the room, were the door facings. Both boards were covered with hash marks that were painstakingly dated. Growth charts for Philip and Desirée, no doubt.

Such a simple, homey little touch that spoke deeply of family and nurturing and milestone moments. The knowledge that those were things he'd never have with his own daughter stabbed at him with a keenness that almost stopped him in his tracks.

Luckily Reeny had her back to him, and he was able to compose himself before she noticed. He stepped into her office and determinedly turned his thoughts to scoping out what the room said about her.

The office was quite small, but clearly all hers. A vintage

wooden table, painted mint green with splashes of white and yellow, served as her desk. An assortment of colorful and obviously kid-crafted pencil holders, coffee mugs, paperweights and other bric-a-brac shared the space with her computer and phone. A matching side table held her printer. A double set of bookcases, the edges painted to complement the desk, lined a nearby wall in easy reach of her desk chair. On it were a hodgepodge of software boxes, tax manuals and reference books all shelved randomly with family pictures and what seemed to be a collection of vintage perfume bottles. A tall file cabinet, which had somehow retained its nondescript beige coloring, sat across the room. On the wall next to it was a wrought-iron cross.

He turned from his survey to find Reeny watching him.

"What do you think?"

"I think it suits you." Colorful and eclectic, putting family and faith front and center, cherishing the traditional but unafraid of the modern—that was Reeny all right.

His answer seemed to confuse her for a moment, but then she moved to the chair behind her desk and turned on the computer. "It'll take me just a few minutes to pull up the site. Any suggestions for how we go about making our picks?"

"Other than Edith's suggestion that we stick to level-one arrangements, I think we just go with what we like. I take it you've already listened to some of them?"

She nodded. "Quite a few actually. I couldn't stop myself."

He liked the way her eyes lit up when she was excited about something. "Then I take it you've already found some you like better than others." When she admitted she had, he continued, "Then why don't we focus on those and go from there?"

Later, when Philip came to the door to tell Reeny that Desirée was ready for bed, Graham was startled to realize it was nine o'clock. No wonder Philip's tone held an accusatory edge.

He stood quickly. "I'm sorry. I didn't mean to stay so late. I think any two of the three we've narrowed it down to will work—I'll let you pick."

Reeny had stood, as well. "No need to apologize. I lost track of time, as well. And I agree with you about any of the three being fine. I just think forcing me to make the final decision is very ungentlemanly of you."

Graham grinned as he moved with her to the hall. "You wound me, madam. I'm only bowing to your right as our esteemed director."

She gave a very unladylike *humph.* "I *knew* there was a reason I didn't want the job."

He laughed outright at that. Then, as they met a droopy-eyed Desirée in the dining room, he waved a hand. "Don't bother seeing me out. I know the way, and you have a sleepy little princess to tuck in."

Desirée gave him a toothy smile, one that ended in a yawn. With a nod to him, Reeny scooped her up and softly stroked her hair.

A few minutes later, as Graham crossed the lawn to his own house, he carried with him the picture of Reeny cradling her daughter in her arms and humming softly.

It stirred both a sense of loss and longings in him that, try as he might, he couldn't seem to quell.

Reeny set her book on the bench, glancing around to check on the kids. Bayou Cigale Park was a popular Saturday morning gathering spot for the preteen set and today was no exception.

Spotting Desirée playing jump rope with two other girls, and Philip trying to teach Buddy a new trick, she let her gaze wander farther afield.

Even though there was still dew on the grass, some local volunteers were hard at work sprucing up the park's pavilion, touching it up with fresh paint and making any needed repairs. The airy, scrollwork-festooned structure would serve as stage and bandstand for the upcoming Labor Day festivities.

Settling more comfortably on the well-worn bench, she lifted her book, then lowered it a moment later when she realized she wasn't taking in any of the words. Her mind kept wandering to other things. Jeff had hung their sign on Thursday and it sure looked nice. Their second practice session had gone well. They were handling the start-up exercises with more confidence and had been enthusiastic about getting to work on the pieces she and Graham had picked out. The exception was Carrie, but Reeny figured that was just natural shyness and that she'd come around soon.

Then there was Graham.

She wasn't quite sure what she felt where he was concerned. She enjoyed his company, of course. But surely it wasn't more than that. After all, she'd only known the man for three weeks. Not nearly time enough to form any sort of deep connection. So why did she get all—

As if her thoughts had conjured him up, Reeny looked closer at the figure jogging along the walking trail. Yep, it was Graham all right. She had to admit, he looked great running so effortlessly, embodying the wholly masculine grace of a tiger in motion.

As she watched, he slowed his pace, gradually winding down to a walk. He spied her and, after what looked like a slight hesitation, altered course in her direction.

"Hi there," she said as he drew near. "You certainly are a dedicated runner to be jogging in this heat."

"Not so much dedicated as addicted." He plopped down on the bench beside her and dragged the cloth off his neck, using it to wipe his forehead. "I'm getting a later than usual start today, but I find I get all kinds of tense and cranky if I miss running too many days in a row."

Cranky, huh? So he didn't maintain that steely control all the time?

"What's going on over there?"

She followed his glance to the activity around the pavilion. "The town likes to spruce things up before the Labor Day festivities."

"Festivities?"

"Uh-huh. Labor Day is a 'big deal' in Tippanyville." She emphasized the words *big deal* with air quotes. "Just about everybody gathers here at the park for what amounts to a town-wide block party."

"Do they, now?"

"Yep. It's not really an organized event—more like a long-standing tradition. Lots of grilling, lots of eating, lots of visiting. Frisbees, kites, horseshoes and volleyballs have even been known to appear from thin air."

"Sounds like a magical event."

She was beginning to really appreciate his dry sense of humor. "Like I said, Tippanyville is all about get-togethers and food. Again, nothing formal, but there are usually several impromptu performances in the bandstand. Sort of like a free-for-all talent show—younger folks with guitars, older folks with fiddles—that sort of thing. And there'll likely be singing, too. If we're lucky, Miss Ada and Miss Clotile will do a couple of numbers."

"You mean sing?"

Reeny nodded. "You'd be surprised at the show those two can put on." She stroked the corner of her mouth. "Maybe next year we can get the Ding-a-lings to perform."

"Yes, maybe *you* can."

She frowned at his emphasis of the word *you*, then shrugged it off. There was still lots of time to convince him he needed the group as much as they needed him. "Anyway, folks usually gather in loose groups of family and friends and stake out one of the picnic tables or spread blankets under the trees as a home base for the day. Which reminds me, if you haven't made plans with another group, you'd be more than welcome to join us."

Reeny did her best to downplay how much she wanted him to come.

Graham was caught off guard by her invitation. "Mind if I ask who 'us' includes?" he asked, trying to buy a little time.

"It'll be me and the kids and my mom, along with Ray's mom and dad. Jake—that's my brother—usually comes but he may or may not make it this year."

She had a brother? "I take it he doesn't live here in Tippanyville."

She shook her head. "He has a law practice up in Alexandria and it keeps him pretty busy. Anyway, since Joscelyn moved back to Tippanyville four years ago she always joins us. And I've invited Andrea and Carrie this year since they're both alone."

Seemed as if Reeny was always taking in strays. Hmm, did that mean she saw him as a stray, as well? Now there was a disturbing thought.

Luckily she seemed entirely unaware of his thoughts. "Actually, you'd be doing me a favor. Since Jake is iffy on whether he can make it, I'm sure Ray's dad would love to have some male company, and you could help him with the grilling."

Ah, so he was merely the token male. That he could handle. "Grilling—that's a whole different story. Mind if I bring my own sauce?"

Her smile brightened. "So you'll come? And yes, feel free to bring your own sauce, but I'll warn you, Ray's dad—just like every other red-blooded Cajun guy in these parts—will defend the superiority of his own recipe against all comers."

"Ah, but St. Louis natives like to think they invented the barbecue. At least the barbecue-done-right."

She grinned. "Them's fighting words around here."

He spread his hands, enjoying the verbal sparring. "You really can't argue with the truth. So what's the usual fare at these picnics?"

"Want to know the menu before you commit, is that it?"

"A man can't be too careful."

"Well, the menu revolves around grilled hamburgers and hot dogs, which of course is the wholly male province. Us womenfolk content ourselves with competing for who can bring the best side dish or dessert."

"All right, I'm convinced. So what do I bring, besides the sauce?"

"Well, Mr. St. Louis-makes-the-best-barbecue, why don't you surprise us with a specialty of your own."

"A challenge, huh? All right, you're on."

"By the way, I know you said you're not much of a church-goer these days, but if you change your mind, you're welcome to go with me and the kids tomorrow. Our preacher is a fine man and I promise you won't be tempted to doze off during his sermon."

And just like that the mood was broken. And he'd really been enjoying her company. Why did she have to keep pushing? Didn't the woman know when to leave well enough alone? "Thanks, but I don't think so."

She didn't seem the least bit fazed by his tone. "The invitation stands, whenever you're ready."

She could wait forever—that was one invitation he didn't plan to accept.

Chapter Fourteen

Reeny glanced at the flag-bedecked pavilion as she carried her second load of food and plasticware to the spot staked out by the Perette-Landry clan. It was only nine-thirty but already a group of senior adults had taken the stage and were singing some old gospel numbers.

A trio of chattering teenagers passed her, closely followed by two men carrying a large cooler between them. The park was really starting to fill up.

She arrived at their spot to find it almost abandoned—only her mother-in-law was there, fussily arranging the food items on the bright, checkered tablecloth.

Shading her hands against the early-morning sun, Reeny spied her mom talking to the Chauquettes over at the next picnic table. Down on the left of the pavilion, where the trees were less dense, Desirée and Pa-paw Woody were trying to get a bright yellow kite in the air.

A quick glance toward Bayou Cigale, near where the old footbridge crossed over, assured her Philip and two of his friends still fished from a borrowed pirogue. The three boys had learned how to handle the shallow boat years ago and they could all swim like tadpoles, but still, it didn't hurt to keep an eye on them.

"That's the last of it," she told Ray's mom as she set her load down. "Can I help you with anything?"

"I think everything's taken care of." Her mother-in-law fussily rearranged a couple of platters, then turned to Reeny. "We haven't had much chance to talk lately. Tell me how that handbell project of yours is doing."

Reeny was almost relieved to have Ray's mom voice the question. She'd been waiting for it ever since her in-laws arrived at the park thirty minutes ago. All the time they'd been setting up the portable grill, unfolding lawn chairs and unpacking hampers, Reeny had braced herself for the inevitable inquisition.

"Actually, we're finally making some real progress. All of the equipment is in, and we started regular practice sessions last week. Oh, and we now have a full complement of eleven members."

"I heard you were directing the group yourself and that Graham Lockwood is lending a hand."

Reeny nodded, unable to tell if there was censure in her tone or not. "Graham has a background in music, so he's been a big help." She nudged one of the food platters a few inches to the right. "We're hoping to be ready to perform at the Fall Festival."

Her mother-in-law raised a brow. "Sounds mighty ambitious."

Reeny's mom had rejoined them during the conversation. "Don't you worry, Lavinia, Reeny and her choir will put on a show that I'm sure would have made that boy of yours proud."

Lavinia's face scrunched up a bit at that, but she settled for responding with a nod and a noncommittal sound.

Joscelyn arrived just then, offering a welcome change of focus.

"So, what did you bring us this year?" Reeny asked, eyeing

the hamper looped over her friend's arm. Joscelyn loved to cook and was forever trying out new recipes on anyone willing to taste.

"An apple cheddar potato salad and a persimmon pickle relish to go with the burgers. Just wait until you taste them."

"Sounds yummy," Lavinia said drily.

Joscelyn laughed. "It is, I promise. You just have to approach it with an open mind."

She set her bowl on the table and sent Reeny a raised-brow look. "So what's this I hear about Graham Lockwood joining us."

Reeny tried for a casual tone. "Oh, you know, he's new to town and didn't have a group of his own."

"I see. Just being neighborly."

Reeny could feel a bit of warmth climb into her cheeks at Joscelyn's knowing look. It was all perfectly innocent, of course, but her friend insisted on giving it a significance it didn't have.

It was a relief to have Carrie and Andrea walk up just then.

Joscelyn left off her teasing and sniffed the air like a coon dog catching a scent. "I smell chocolate," she declared.

"Must be the chocolate chocolate chip cookies I brought," Carrie answered.

Andrea lifted the box she was carrying. "And I brought a peach-and-blueberry cobbler."

"Oh, girls," Estelle said with a fake groan, "I've gained five pounds just hearing about your food. Go and set those diet-sabotaging goodies on the table with the rest of the food."

All the while they were chatting, Reeny scanned the crowd for signs of Graham. Where was he? Had he changed his mind? Or maybe he didn't realize the Labor Day picnic was an all-day event, not just a lunchtime one. Not that she was anxious or anything. She just didn't like to think of anyone spending the day alone when they could be part of this celebration.

She surreptitiously glanced at her watch. Ten o'clock. Plenty of time for him to join them yet.

"Looks like Desirée and Woody finally got that kite up."

Reeny followed Lavinia's gaze and saw the bright yellow kite was bobbing up in the air. "It was so nice of y'all to get that kite for Desirée."

Lavinia tried to look nonchalant, but failed. "You know how Woody is with kids. Especially that *chère bébé* granddaughter of ours."

Some of Reeny's earlier tension eased. This was more like the way things were before the issue of how to spend the memorial money had come between them. Maybe she and Ray's mom could eventually get past their differences.

When Reeny finally glanced back around, she spotted Graham crossing the park with that long, graceful stride that no doubt came from his daily jogging routine. He appeared to be dragging a wheeled cooler behind him.

"Sorry I'm late," he said as he reached them. "I wasn't sure just where y'all gathered and ended up parking over on the Azalea Street side." He set the cooler next to the one that was already beside the grill. "Apparently everyone else knew where to find you, though. All sorts of helpful folks gave me directions."

Reeny laughed. "I'm afraid we're creatures of habit— everybody gravitates to the same spot year after year. Just like church folk who sit in the same pew every Sunday." She eyed his cooler. "What do we have here?"

"I thought I'd contribute some soft drinks, and—" he flipped open the lid with a flourish "—a dozen skewers of marinated surf-and-turf kabobs."

Feeling a bit self-conscious after Joscelyn's teasing, Reeny held back. Joscelyn, however, had no such reservations. She marched over and peered inside. "Yum, look at the size of those shrimp. If you're going to bring food like this, you're definitely drafted to join our group every Labor Day."

"You might want to hold off on that invite until you taste them," he said drily. He caught Reeny's eye and smiled a greeting. And suddenly any awkwardness she'd been feeling evaporated.

Reeny's father-in-law rejoined them, and Graham stepped forward to introduce himself.

"Good to have another man in the group," Woody said, shaking his hand. "I was beginning to feel like the Lone Ranger."

"More than happy to be your Tonto for the day, sir. Just let me know what I can do to help."

The two men began to discuss the relative merits of charcoal versus wood chips and the thick honey-and-brown-sugar-flavored sauce Woody used versus the thinner vinegar-and-soy-flavored sauce Graham had brought.

As the women wandered back to sit around the picnic table, Reeny felt a little spark of something she didn't try to identify. Graham fit right in with their less-than-homogenous group. Almost as if he belonged there.

"I've got the munchies," Joscelyn said. "I vote for breaking out Andrea's salsa and chips."

"Help yourself," Andrea said as she pushed a platter toward them.

"Hey!" Woody waved a long-handled spatula at them. "Don't you gals be eating all the good stuff while us menfolk sweat over this hot grill."

"You mean the way you munched on popcorn while I cooked supper last night," Lavinia replied a bit too sweetly.

"Give it up." Graham offered Reeny's father-in-law a cola. "This is one argument you'll never win."

Lavinia pointed toward the pavilion. "Oh look, Randall is

pulling out his fiddle, and it looks like his granddaughter is going to sing. I think I'll move closer so I can hear better."

Reeny's mom moved around the table. "I'll go with you. We'll leave these girls to their snacks."

Once they'd gone, Joscelyn plucked a cheese straw out of the bowl and waved it like a pointer. "Just think, ladies. Next year the Ding-a-lings might be able to claim a spot on the platform."

Reeny gave her a shoulder bump. "What do you mean *might?*"

Joscelyn popped the cheese straw in her mouth. "Silly me, you're right. They'll probably be asking for us by name."

"Better believe it."

Graham wandered over and snagged a cookie. "I see you ladies have this food monitoring job under control."

He seemed different today, more relaxed, less closed off. She liked this new side of him. He glanced her way and she felt her cheeks heat at having been caught staring. "So how did you two grill masters reconcile the sauce standoff?" she asked quickly.

Graham saw the pink creep into Reeny's cheeks and hid a grin. Nice to know he could still fluster a woman occasionally. "We compromised, like the mature adults we are. We'll use my sauce on all but two of the skewers and on a couple of the burgers. The rest will have his sauce."

"Hey, look," Joscelyn interrupted, pointing toward the pavilion. "Ada and Clotile are lining up to go next."

"Wonder what they put together this year?" Anticipation colored Andrea's voice.

Before he could ask Andrea what she meant, Joscelyn, Andrea and Carrie were headed off toward the pavilion. Which left him and Reeny alone at the table.

Reeny stood. "Come on, you won't want to miss this."

Graham hesitated, glancing toward Woody. But Reeny's father-in-law waved him on. "Go enjoy yourself. I can handle this. Besides, I see Philip headed this way. He's old enough for me to teach him how to turn a burger."

"So," Graham said as he fell into step beside Reeny, "what makes this particular performance so special?"

"Miss Ada and Miss Clotile have been performing duets as far back as I can remember. They sing a cappella, and for a couple of petite ladies they can really belt it out. Just wait until you hear them."

He was having a hard time picturing those two sixty-some-odd-year-olds putting on a performance worthy of this kind of attention.

As if reading his thoughts, Reeny laughed. "I won't say anything more, except that they always add a generous dollop of lagniappe to their performances."

Graham cut her a questioning look, but she just shook her head. "Patience—it's worth the wait."

She was definitely in high spirits—a mood that looked good on her. As they made their way across the park, they were jostled by the crowd and Reeny bumped into him. Their shoulders and arms touched, a perfectly mundane contact that nevertheless heightened his senses, making him more aware of her nearness, of the color in her cheeks, of the subtle, utterly feminine scent that seemed to be a part of her. What had happened to his ability to distance himself?

By the time the two of them joined the crowd gathered around the pavilion, he was more than ready to focus on something else. The unlikely duo had taken the stage and struck an exaggeratedly prim pose. Ada raised a hand for silence, Clotile pulled out a pitch pipe and blew a short blast. They then hummed a few bars of a tune Graham recognized as "My Favorite Things"—not a particularly challenging number.

But when they started singing, he did a double take. Except for the chorus, they'd replaced all the lyrics, gleefully singing lines such as

> *Tabasco in gumbo and spicy boiled crawfish*
> *Swamp mist on thistles and crispy fried catfish*
> *Herons that spring from the pond on spread wings...*

Graham listened, a smile playing on his lips. Reeny was right, they were good. And to add to the fun, they swayed and sashayed to the lyrics with all the gusto of schoolgirls. When they'd finished, he applauded as heartily as anyone.

Reeny gave him a what-did-I-tell-you look.

"I would've never guessed," he acknowledged. "But those two make a great act."

"This is just a sample. They always do something fabulous for the Fall Festival."

Ada and Clotile raised their hands, waiting for the applause to die down. Apparently they were prepared to do a second number. But for this one, they visibly switched gears, taking a more serious stance. As soon as they started, Graham recognized the poignant old hymn, "It Is Well with My Soul." Their rendition was beautiful—reverent, pitch-perfect, powerful.

Graham steadfastly ignored the insistent little tug he felt from somewhere deep inside, telling himself he could appreciate the beauty of their performance without buying into the message of the words. It was only when they finished that he realized he'd curled his hands into tightly clenched fists at his side.

He again joined in the applause as the duo took their final bow and yielded the pavilion stage to three young men with acoustic guitars.

"So, what did you think?" Reeny asked.

"Definitely a unique performance." The hymn was still echoing in his head.

"Unique certainly describes those two." She sighed. "That hymn is one of my very favorites. I've always thought the message was simple and profound at the same time. And that was even before I learned the history behind it."

He knew the story, too, the story of one man's acceptance of God's goodness even in the face of horrific tragedy. Perhaps Mr. Spafford's faith was stronger than his own. Or perhaps the man had merely clung to whatever comfort he could find.

Reeny gave him a sideways glance. "What about you? As a former church choir director, you must have a favorite hymn."

He resisted, then shrugged. After all, he *had* had a favorite. "'The Solid Rock.'"

She nodded. "Another powerful song, with a stirring message."

Not a very subtle woman.

Joscelyn joined them. "That Ada and Clotile are a class act, all the way."

Graham turned, glad for the excuse to focus elsewhere. "It definitely had to be seen—or should I say, heard—to be appreciated."

Estelle strolled up. "Lavinia and I are heading back to the table to check on the food. And on Woody."

"If you'll allow me to join you ladies." Graham offered an arm to each of them. "I was just heading back myself to see if Woody needed any help." And to put some distance between himself and Reeny's all-too-distracting company.

Reeny set her fork down with a groan. "God bless the cooks. Everything was fabulous. I just wish I hadn't tried to taste all of it—I think I'm going to explode."

As if waiting for her pronouncement, Philip pushed back from the table. "Can I go back out on the pirogue with Robby and C.J.?"

"May I," Reeny corrected.

Philip rolled his eyes, but obediently repeated "May I?"

"Clean up your place first. All the paper plates and food scraps need to make it to the trash can."

"Yes, ma'am." Philip worked double-time, even volunteering to carry several other paper plates to the nearby trash receptacle while he was at it. As soon as Reeny gave him the thumbs-up, he raced off to the pirogue.

Desirée tugged on Reeny's shirt, then signed a question.

Reeny shook her head. "No, sweetie, you can't go with your brother."

Desirée's mouth turned down in a pout and she quickly signed a response.

Reeny, remembering her own desire to follow Jake around at that age, tried to soften her refusal. "Because there's no room for you." She gave her daughter an encouraging smile. "As soon as I'm done helping clean up, you and I can grab the Frisbee and toss it around for a while."

Unfortunately, that answer didn't bring Desirée's smile back.

Graham came around the table and plopped down on the bench next to Desirée. His shoulder brushed against Reeny's arm, and she wondered if that had been deliberate. "Hey, munchkin," he said, "have you ever built a paper boat?"

Desirée gave him a suspicious look as she shook her head.

"You haven't?" Graham seemed taken aback. "We've got to remedy that. How about you and I construct us each one right now?"

She shrugged, then nodded.

Graham seemed undeterred by her less than enthusiastic response. He turned to Reeny. "I assume you have your notebook with you even here?"

"Won't leave home without it." She grabbed her tote bag, pulled out her pad and handed it to Graham.

He opened it up and turned to the first blank page then looked up at her. "May I?" When she nodded he tore out two sheets and handed one to Desirée. "Now, you just do what I do and you'll have yourself a sweet little boat in no time. My dad taught me how to do this when I was just about your age."

As the grown-ups continued lazily cleaning up from the meal, Reeny surreptitiously kept an eye on the two bent heads. Graham patiently demonstrated the folding technique to her daughter, praising her efforts without once speaking down to her. It didn't take long for Desirée to respond to his efforts.

At one point Graham looked up and caught her watching. This time, instead of feeling embarrassed, she mouthed a simple "Thank you." To her surprise, he winked and then bent down to demonstrate the next fold.

When they were done, he studied both boats, then frowned. "A proper boat needs a name. Don't you agree?"

Desirée nodded and Graham pulled a pen out of his pocket. "I think I'll name mine Champ."

Predictably, Desirée wrote Buddy on the side of hers. When she was done, she went around showing it off proudly to everyone still at the table. Reeny could have hugged Graham for putting the smile back on her daughter's face.

"It's beautiful, sweetie," she said when Desirée held it up to her. "I'll bet Philip is going to want you to teach him how to make one when he sees it."

Graham stood. "What do you say we go down to the bayou and see if these will float?"

Desirée nodded. She skipped to his side and held out a hand.

Reeny saw the flash of surprise cross Graham's face before he took it in his much larger one and strolled beside her to the bayou.

Something inside her fluttered to life as she studied the picture they made.

Joscelyn slipped up beside her. "Now there's a man who needs a few kids of his own," she whispered.

Before she could catch herself, Reeny nodded.

Let Joscelyn read into that whatever she wanted.

Chapter Fifteen

Thursday morning Reeny glanced at her watch as she strolled down the student-filled hallway. She had a few minutes before it was time to go over to Dominick's restaurant and go over his books with him, just enough time to stop in and say hi to Joscelyn.

Tuesday's practice had gone really well—the group was making progress in both technical skill and in pulling together as a group. Miss Ada had brought the promised curtains for the windows—Kelly green with a pair of gold handbells appliquéd on each panel to match the ones Andrea had carved on the wooden sign. The whole choir had hung around after practice to help hang them.

With the Labor Day festivities still fresh on everyone's mind, Reeny had broached the subject of performing at the Fall Festival, downplaying the formal performance aspect and focusing on the let's-have-something-fun-to-aim-for aspect. After some initial hesitation, the group had come around, enthusiastically endorsing the idea and talking about uniforms. They'd settled on black pants, a white shirt and green bow ties to match the new curtains.

Yep, it had been a very good session.

Just as Reeny reached the office, someone hailed her. Turning, she saw her mother-in-law headed her way. And Lavinia did *not* look happy.

"Is it true, what I heard?"

Uh-oh, what now? Reeny tried a cheery smile. "That depends, what did you hear?"

Lavinia's expression didn't soften. "That you named that handbell choir of yours the Ding-a-lings." She said the name as if it was an epithet.

"That's right. I thought it was sort of fun and playful."

"How could you? This was supposed to be a memorial to Ray."

"It is. But—"

"And do you think that's the proper way to honor his memory—with some *bête* group called Ding-a-lings? I thought you'd at least have the decency to include his name."

Lavinia's complexion had turned alarmingly red and students were beginning to take notice. "I'm sorry it upset you." Reeny kept her tone soft and conciliatory. "But Ray had such a wonderful sense of humor—that's one of the things people always loved about him. I know if you stop and think for a minute you'll see this is just the kind of wordplay he would have loved."

"But this is not supposed to be about what *he* loved." Ray's mom took a deep breath, as if fighting some strong emotion. "It's supposed to be about leaving a legacy to remember him by." Without another word, she brushed past Reeny and marched down the hall, her back boat-paddle stiff.

Reeny's shoulders slumped. This wonderful, God-sent opportunity should have brought her and Ray's mom closer together. Instead it was having the opposite effect. Would the two of them ever be able to get past this?

She turned to find Joscelyn standing in the office doorway. How much had she heard?

"Oh, hi." She tried to shake off the confused, flustered feeling and pull herself together. "Sorry, can't chat right now. I've got an appointment—"

"Are you okay?"

"I'm fine. Just in a bit of a hurry."

"Your appointment will wait. Come with me."

"No, really, I—"

But Joscelyn wasn't taking no for an answer. She grabbed Reeny's elbow and all but dragged her into her office, not letting go until Reeny plopped down in one of the guest chairs. Then she pulled a bottle of water out of her desk drawer. "Here, drink this."

Reeny unscrewed the cap and took a long swig. When she'd swallowed she met her friend's concerned gaze. "So, I guess you overheard."

Joscelyn folded her arms. "Yes."

Reeny looked away, fiddling with the neck of the water bottle. "I should have realized how she would take this. I should have been more sensitive to—"

"Reeny, there's nothing you need to apologize to *anyone* for."

"Thanks, but you don't have to try to make me feel better."

Joscelyn made an exasperated sound. "If you're looking to lay guilt, I should take a boatload of it myself."

Reeny looked up. "What? This has nothing to do with you—"

"Oh, doesn't it? Did you or did you not come up with this project to provide a ministry for hurting individuals? And was I or was I not one of the first people you thought of?"

Had she been that transparent? "Joscelyn, I never—"

Her friend waved a hand, dismissing her concern. "Oh, don't worry, I don't think anyone else has connected the dots in quite that way, but I know you pretty well, *chère*. And don't get me wrong, I'm very glad you came up with this particular plan. Which, I suppose, makes me quite selfish. So don't go gathering up all the blame for yourself." Then she grinned. "Besides, what you told Lavinia is true. I can just see Ray getting a big old kick out of you and me being part of a group called the Ding-a-lings."

Reeny felt an answering grin tug at her lips. "Wouldn't he just." But her grin faded as she remembered the anger and hurt in her mother-in-law's face. "I just hate the wedge this is driving between Ray's mom and me. She's a *good* person and she still misses Ray with the ache only a mother could feel. I can't stand the thought that I'm adding to her pain."

Joscelyn leaned forward and grasped both her hands. "*You* are not adding to her pain. This is something she's going to have to work through for herself. And she'll probably come around once she sees the choir become a reality."

Reeny wasn't so sure. "Well, that's enough self-pity from me for one day." Not that she believed for one minute that she couldn't have handled things better. But she smiled brightly as she stood. "Thanks for both the water and the pep talk. And I really do need to go now or Dominick's going to wonder if his bookkeeper absconded with his books."

Graham arrived at the practice session early that evening. He'd heard what had passed between Reeny and Lavinia and, knowing Reeny, he could imagine how upset she'd been by it. She probably needed a bit of a morale boost.

Slamming shut the door of his SUV, he strode up the walk and shoved open the building's door. A quick look around showed Mrs. Perette and Reeny's two kids setting out the bells, while Reeny stood at the counter jotting something in her notebook. Good, he could talk to her privately without being too obvious.

He returned the greetings from the three at work on the bells but headed straight for Reeny, studying her demeanor. She'd glanced up when the shop bell jingled, and as far as he could tell there were no obvious signs of distress. But she wasn't fooling him.

"I heard what happened at school today," he said when he reached her. "Are you all right?"

She glanced across the room, as if worried the others had overheard his comment. But he'd been careful to pitch his voice for her ears only.

"I'm fine." She flashed a smile as if trying to prove her point. Then she sobered. "So, how far has the story spread?"

He shrugged, trying to downplay the situation. "You know how these things go."

She grimaced. "That bad, huh?"

At least she seemed to be taking it well. "By tomorrow there'll be some other brouhaha for folks to discuss and it'll be forgotten."

She nodded. "You're probably right. There's nothing I can do about it anyway."

He sensed a fragileness about her that tugged at him. "Do you want me to take the lead today?" he asked impulsively.

Surprise flashed across her face, and he could almost feel some of her tension ease. It made him somewhat ashamed that he'd been so hard-nosed about making her always take the lead.

"Thanks, but I'm fine, really." Her soft tone was almost a caress. Then she closed her notebook and took a deep breath. "I mean, I'm sorry Ray's mom is upset. I feel guilty that I didn't realize this would hurt her. But I can't turn back the clock." She fiddled with her locket. "I'll just have to try to be more sensitive to her feelings and put the rest in God's hands."

Jeff and Mark arrived just then, closely followed by Dana, so there was no further opportunity for private conversation.

He watched her all through the session and couldn't detect any cracks in her humor and patience. Except perhaps that her smile was just the slightest bit fixed. And there was a hint of tired circles under her eyes.

Except when she met his gaze. Then her expression softened and she seemed to get a fresh burst of energy. It made him feel as if he were really helping her somehow, as if there were a connection between the two of them.

He told himself it was just because he'd shown support earlier, that it was one friend being there for another.

He wouldn't let himself consider that it was anything more.

Graham exited the hardware store Friday afternoon and almost literally bumped into Reeny and her two kids. From the look of the bag she held, they'd just come out of the restaurant next door.

"Decided to take a break from cooking tonight, I see." He searched her face for signs of the strain that had been there yesterday evening. Other than a bit of tiredness in her eyes, she seemed in better spirits.

She nodded. "It's muffy and movie night."

"Beg pardon?"

Reeny laughed. "Most Fridays the kids and I come down to Dominick's for muffuletta sandwiches, then we rent a movie and go home and have movie night."

"Sounds like fun." He had a quick vision of the empty house he was headed home to.

"You're welcome to join us."

Had she read his thoughts? "I wasn't wrangling for an invitation."

"Don't be silly. The more the merrier. In fact Joscelyn is supposed to come over tonight, so you won't be the only one. And sometimes Mom will drop in, as well. I always have a few extra muffuletta quarters on hand, just in case."

Her cell phone rang and she hurriedly shoved the food at Philip while she dug into her tote. When she hung up she looked back at Graham. "Well, that cinches it. Joscelyn can't make it tonight so we need someone else to eat her portion."

Graham found himself the focus of three pairs of eyes. "One question—what's a muffuletta sandwich?"

Reeny melodramatically placed one hand over her heart and touched her cheek with the other. "Are you telling me you've *never* tasted a muffuletta? No doubt about it now. You have to come over so we can introduce you to this culinary treat."

The invitation did sound much more inviting than his empty house. Besides, it wouldn't hurt to make sure she wasn't just putting a happy face on her hurt. "Count me in. So what's the movie?"

"An old Landry family favorite—the original *Stars Wars* movie. Don't be surprised if Philip parrots some of the lines along with the characters or if he and Desirée act out some of the scenes."

"Mo-om." Philip's voice had that you're-embarrassing-me pitch to it.

"Sorry, kiddo." She bumped him with her hip. "But you know I love you anyway."

This time Philip just rolled his eyes.

Reeny laughed then turned back to Graham, her dimple still on display. "The movie goes in the DVD player at six-thirty."

"What can I bring?"

"Don't worry about that. Muffulettas do a good job of filling you up, believe me."

Graham arrived ten minutes before movie time. She was in the kitchen unwrapping the sandwiches while the kids were pulling out paper plates and plastic cups. She glanced at the bag in his hand and shook her head in mock concern. "Your grandmother's teaching must go very deep."

"You have no idea." He shook the bag. "I stopped at the store and picked up some malted milk balls—my all-time favorite movie theater treat."

Philip responded with an enthusiastic "Oh boy," and

Desirée did a little skip step. Reeny, however, got a Cheshire-cat grin as she reached into a cabinet and pulled out a tray. "I'm beginning to get the feeling the Landrys aren't the only ones with a taste for chocolate."

Okay, maybe she *was* fully recovered. "I have no idea what you mean," he said piously. Then he set the bag down and rubbed his hands together. "What can I do to help?"

She handed him the tray and a roll of paper towels. "Here, line this and arrange the sandwiches on it. Desirée, get the chips please. Philip, if you'll carry the paper plates and cups, I'll get the jug of tea."

A muffuletta, it turned out, was a sandwich made with a round, plate-size loaf of bread sliced like a hamburger bun and piled high with several types of Italian meats and cheeses which were in turn topped with an olive salad mixture.

She had purchased two of the huge sandwiches and Graham obediently placed all eight of the burger-size quarters on the tray.

Everything was carried into the den and deposited on the coffee table. The kids plopped down on the floor where Buddy joined them, while Reeny and Graham took the sofa.

There was enough room between them to seat another person, but he still was hyperaware of her every shift, every breath. He knew the two of them would likely never be more than friends. Still, he couldn't help but wonder what would it be like to place his arm around her shoulders, to tuck her head protectively against his chest, to keep all the people that would hurt her at bay?

And how would she react if he tried?

Reeny had the kitchen to herself. Graham had left twenty minutes ago and the kids were getting ready for bed. It had been a fun evening, a much-needed bit of playtime after the stressful run-in with her mother-in-law yesterday.

But now she was feeling a different kind a tension, a con-usion she didn't know how to deal with. Was it possible her eelings for Graham went deeper than mere friendship? She ad no experience with men other than Ray. He'd been her igh school sweetheart, the only boy she'd ever dated. And fter his passing she'd been so busy reshaping her world for erself and her kids that she'd had no time for other men. And o real interest.

Until now.

It was as if something inside her had awakened after a long leep. Not necessarily that she was in love. Just that she was eady to take notice and think about the possibility again.

Heavenly Father, I know You put Graham in my life—or e in his—for a reason. I'm going to take this slow and easy, ut please help me to discover what Your purpose is.

Chapter Sixteen

When Carrie arrived at practice Monday evening she made a beeline for Reeny. "I need to talk to you."

"Of course." Reeny led her to a spot near the counter that was relatively private, wondering what was up. Carrie seemed more fidgety than usual. "Is something the matter?"

"Yes and no." Carrie fiddled with the handle of her purse. "Look, Reeny, I know what you're trying to do with this choir, and I really appreciate that you invited me to be a part of it."

Apparently Joscelyn hadn't been the only one to figure out her motives. "But?"

"But—and please don't take this the wrong way—this is not what I need right now."

Before Reeny could say anything, Carrie rushed on. "I moved to Tippanyville when I married Doug nine years ago, and I love the people here, but I've always felt more of a guest than family, if you know what I mean." She shifted her weight. "It's as much me as anyone—I just don't make friends easily. But to be honest, without Doug here this no longer feels like home."

Feelings of failure, understanding, what-ifs flashed through Reeny. "So you're moving."

Carrie nodded. "I've been talking to my cousin Marty back in Vicksburg. She's alone too and she invited me to move in with her. I think a fresh start and a change of scene will be good for me."

"We'll miss you."

"I know, and I feel awful about leaving y'all in the lurch this way."

Reeny took Carrie's hands in her own. "No, I mean we'll miss *you*. I wish you nothing but happiness, and I'll be praying you find what you're looking for."

Carrie stepped up and hugged her. "I can't thank you enough. These past three weeks have meant more to me than you'll ever know. It got me out of that empty house and pulled me out of my wallowing self-pity so I could figure out how to move on." She cleared her throat nervously. "Will you say my goodbyes to everyone for me? I don't think I could handle that right now."

"Of course." Reeny pulled her bottom lip between her teeth as she watched Carrie hurry away.

Was there something more she could have, should have done? If she'd gotten the choir up and running sooner. If she'd found ways to spend time with Carrie outside of choir practice…

Graham joined her at the counter and nodded toward the door. "Carrie not joining us today?"

"No." She took a deep breath and blurted out what had to be said. "You were right. She won't be continuing with the choir."

Graham lightly touched her arm. "I'm sorry."

At least he didn't lead with I told you so. "No, it's okay. I think she's going to be all right." Recalling the way Carrie's face had lit up when she talked about returning to Vicksburg, Reeny suddenly believed her own words.

"She's moving back to her hometown to live with a cousin. The clean break and family connections will be good for her."

"Glad to hear it. But it sounds like we're going to be one choir member short."

"I know. And we're only seven weeks away from the Fall Festival. It's going to be hard to pull someone new in at this point and have them up to speed in time for the performance."

Graham nodded. "Geralyn and Mark are our two strongest ringers. Maybe we could get one of them to cover both—"

"I'll do it."

Reeny turned around to find her mom standing behind her. "Mom?"

Estelle pushed her glasses up higher on her nose. "Sorry to be eavesdropping, but I saw Carrie leave and wondered what was wrong. I know I'm not the ideal candidate, but I've been watching your practice sessions, so I wouldn't be starting completely from scratch. Maybe with a little extra tutoring on the side from one of you two I can catch up to the others. And since I'm here at every session anyway…"

"Are you sure, Mom?"

"Yes. Just to get you through the Fall Festival, though. That'll give you plenty of time to recruit a more permanent replacement."

Reeny gave her hands a squeeze. "You're a lifesaver."

Then she turned to Graham. "If you'll work with her one-on-one, I'll get everyone else started on the group exercises."

Graham smiled at their newest recruit. "It'll be my pleasure."

Graham slid the last of the instrument cases into the cabinet while Reeny shelved the music binders.

"I'll practice a few hours with Mom while the kids are in school the next few days," Reeny said. "I can use the extra time on the instruments myself."

"She's quick." Graham closed the cabinet. "And determined. With a little extra help I think she'll catch up with the others in no time."

"Wouldn't surprise me a bit. Sometimes I think Mom can do anything she sets her mind to."

Like mother, like daughter.

She gave him a quizzical look. "What about you? I hear you talk about your grandmother but not your parents."

Surprisingly, her question didn't seem like prying. In fact, he found himself ready to share a little bit of his history with her. "My parents died when I was nine and my mother's parents took me in and raised me. Granddad died of a heart attack about eight years ago and Nana followed two years later, almost to the day."

"I'm sorry."

"Nana was a real character, one of the strongest, most grounded women I ever knew. The adages that anything worth doing is worth doing well and that simple pleasures are the best kind were not just words to her—they were ways of life. She always believed a body should earn his keep, but she'd give you her last penny if she thought you needed it."

"Sounds like quite a woman."

"She was. I still find myself wanting to turn to her for advice from time to time." Like when he'd lost Annie…

He shook that thought off. "Back to the choir. I think it might be a good idea to recruit at least one new member. That way we have a little more shuffling room if someone else has to pull out, and you have someone ready to step in when your mother bows out after the festival."

"I'll start putting out feelers." She reached for her tote, pulled out her ever-present tablet and scratched out a few quick notes. "Speaking of the festival, do you think we ought to practice both of the numbers each session or would it be better to concentrate on one until…"

Graham let Reeny talk, making appropriate responses when she paused for his input. He was still mulling over her reaction to Carrie's departure from the group. The woman was not only able to roll with even the hardest of punches, but at the same time she continued to see everything through those rose-colored glasses of hers.

At one time he considered her to be foolishly Pollyan-naish. But he was coming to see it as an area of strength—a strength that not only kept her from breaking, but one that she was able to share with others when they needed it.

He only hoped it didn't fail her, because if it did, she would fall hard. He had some experience with that.

And he couldn't bear the thought of it happening to her.

So far, most of the effort in building up their friendship had come from her. Time to show her he would be there for her if she needed him.

Chapter Seventeen

At the sound of the knock, Reeny set her cup of coffee down next to the open newspaper. Who could that be this early on a Saturday morning? She opened the kitchen door to find Graham standing there, dressed for his run.

"Hi, neighbor," he said cheerily.

"Oh, hi." She was suddenly acutely aware that she had her hair gathered messily on the back of her head and that she was wearing the old T-shirt and frayed jeans she donned for housework. "Can I offer you a cup of coffee?"

"No thanks, I'm headed over to the park." He didn't attempt to enter. "I just wanted to check in and see if you had any plans for this afternoon."

His question caught her off guard. What was he up to? "Why, no. Nothing special anyway. Just planning to catch up on some of my bookkeeping."

"Good. Because I've decided it's high time I start repaying that considerable debt I owe you."

Had she missed something? "And what debt is that?"

"By my reckoning, you've fed me no less than three times." He held up three fingers for emphasis. "And all I have on my side of the ledger is a couple of measly store-bought pizzas. So, if you and the kids don't have any objections, I thought I'd break out the old grill and cook us up some burgers."

"Oh for goodness' sake, no one's keeping count. You don't have to—"

He held up a hand to halt her protest and she laughed. "Oh. Your grandmother's strictures again."

"Exactly." He shrugged. "What can I say? I'm a creature of my upbringing."

"In that case, the kids and I would love to join you for hamburgers this afternoon."

"Great. I plan to fire up the grill around four-thirty but feel free to come on over whenever you're ready." With a wave, he headed off toward his SUV.

Reeny closed the door and drifted back to her coffee. But rather than picking up the newspaper she stared at nothing in particular. She tried not to read anything into his invitation other than neighborliness. Still, regardless of his motives, her mood had lightened considerably.

Reeny and the kids, with Buddy at their heels, followed the scent of burning hickory chips around to Graham's backyard.

"Ah, there you are." Graham waved them over with a long-handled spatula. "And bearing gifts I see."

Reeny nodded. "I've got baked beans and Desirée's carrying a platter of chocolate chip cookies." She raised a brow. "Yours wasn't the only grandmother to give lessons on proper etiquette, you know. Of course, in my case it was my mother rather than my grandmother."

"Where would we be without mothers and grandmothers to set us on the right path?"

"Amen." She held up the bowl. "Shall I set this in the kitchen?"

"Good idea. But you, young lady," he waved the spatula from Desirée to the patio table, "set those cookies right over there so I can keep an eye on them."

Desirée grinned at his theatrics and set the platter where he'd instructed.

Graham proved to be an excellent host. He kept them entertained with stories of his childhood growing up on his grandparents' farm.

There was a dicey moment when the food was served and Graham reached for his fork. Philip looked at him with a frown. "Aren't you going to ask the blessing, Mr. Lockwood?"

He hesitated a moment, and Reeny held her breath.

Then he nodded. "Of course." Bowing his head, he offered up his prayer in a clear, strong voice. "Dear God, we thank You for this food and for the good friends gathered here to share it with. Keep us always in Your care. Amen."

Once they all repeated the amen, Reeny caught his gaze and smiled. He nodded and turned to serve Desirée a burger.

She knew that hadn't been comfortable for him, but it hadn't showed. She could also tell he'd been a praying man at one time. And perhaps he would be again.

With a smile and a silent prayer of her own, she settled in to enjoy Graham's burgers.

At the end of the meal, Desirée turned to Graham, signing a request to build paper boats again, a request Philip seconded. Pulling a stack of paper from his printer, Graham spent the next thirty minutes showing them a number of variations on the folding technique he'd shown Desirée on Labor Day. From there they moved on to paper airplanes and the evening ended with a fierce competition to see whose plane could fly the farthest.

Reeny watched them as she took her time picking up after

the meal. Jake had filled the father-figure role for Philip and Desirée for a while after Ray died. But he wasn't able to come around as much now as he had in the past.

Having Graham in their lives helped fill that gap, even if in a small way. Did he know how big a part of their lives, *all* of their lives, he was becoming?

Graham waited until the Landrys were inside their own home before he switched off the yard lights. He wandered into the living room, plopped down in his easy chair and switched on the television. There was a football game on but he didn't even notice which teams were playing.

He'd had a good time this afternoon. Reeny was easy to talk to and her kids were great.

Philip was a bit standoffish, but that wasn't out of the ordinary for students who had to interact with their teacher outside the classroom. He was making some headway with the boy. In fact he'd seemed to thaw a bit today when they were working on the paper boats and planes.

And Desirée was a little sweetheart. She could melt your heart with just a smile.

Yep, tonight had been a success on all fronts. It had shown that he and the Landrys could be good friends and neighbors, could have fun evenings together, could enjoy each other's company and not have to take it any further than that.

Sort of like having your cake and eating it, too. Exactly what he'd come here looking for.

Now if he could just get over that something's-missing feeling.

There was an after-school faculty meeting on Monday. When it was finally over, Graham headed straight for the parking lot. He had some papers to get graded before choir practice this afternoon.

Fred Gros, another faculty member, fell into step beside him. "Hey, I hear you got roped into helping Reeny with her handbell choir scheme."

Graham wasn't sure he cared for Fred's tone. "I wouldn't say I was roped in. I volunteered to help her out."

"Oh, you don't have to be politically correct with me. I not only grew up with her but I'm Ray's cousin—I know how hard it can be to say no to her when she has her mind set."

"I happen to enjoy music," Graham said evenly.

Fred laughed. "But that's not real music, right? She's got everyone clanging bells, like those Santas at the mall during Christmas time. I mean, I even hear they're calling themselves the Ding-a-lings. How's anyone supposed to take 'em seriously with a name like that?"

No, he definitely didn't like the man's tone. "Have you ever actually *heard* a handbell choir perform?"

Fred shrugged, his smile fading. "No. But I don't care how good it sounds. It's just a real shame Reeny wouldn't listen to reason. I mean, that money could've done this town some good if she hadn't been so stubborn."

"It was her decision to make," Graham said firmly. "And I'm sure she made the one she thought best." He'd finally reached his vehicle and he pulled open the door. "And I happen to agree with her." He held Fred's gaze a moment longer with every ounce of authority he could command, then slid inside and closed the door on the man's surprised frown.

Turning the key in the ignition, Graham worked at easing some of the tenseness from his muscles, especially his jaw. Was this the kind of badgering Reeny had had to put up with? Sure, she'd mentioned some opposition to her plans and he knew how Lavinia felt, but he hadn't realized just how in-your-face it actually was.

How in the world had she managed to hold on to her good humor and optimism, not to mention temper, when faced with this?

Graham didn't mention anything to Reeny about his encounter with Fred. It wouldn't serve any useful purpose and would only give her something else to worry about. Instead, he did his best to keep the mood upbeat at the practice session that evening.

Toward the end of the session, they did a run-through of the first number they were scheduled to perform at the Fall Festival. When they finished, Reeny started clapping. "That was amazing. The town is in for a lovely surprise when we get up on that stage in just five short weeks." She closed her notebook. "And I think on that note we'll call it a night."

As usual, there was a lot of lingering to talk and visit a while after practice. The five-short-weeks comment had stirred everyone up, which he suspected had been Reeny's intention.

By the time everyone left, Graham was sliding the last of the instrument cases into the cabinet.

"So," he said, leaning back against the wall, "what was that all about?"

She started shelving the binders. "What was what all about?"

"Don't act wide-eyed and innocent. You deliberately got everyone stirred up about the amount of time left before the festival. I thought you wanted them to focus on fun and fellowship."

"Part of that fellowship is a feeling of responsibility toward each other. Lately I get the impression Dana and Mark are more concerned about their art project than about the choir. And some of the others are getting lax. I figure a little nudge won't hurt anyone."

So, there was a touch of steel under that soft exterior, was there?

"By the way," she added, "I think I may have found us another recruit. Her name is Colette Ramey—Lettie for short."

"Don't think I know her."

"She's the local beautician. Anyway, I think she'd be a good fit for the group, but I'm trying to figure out whether to bring her in now or wait until after the festival. What do you think?"

He liked that she sought his opinion before making a decision about the group. While they discussed the pros and cons, Graham retrieved the toolbox he'd left here the evening they'd hung Ada's curtains. There were a few fix-it jobs at the house that needed his attention.

During their discussion, Reeny made a passing reference to her mother-in-law, which put Graham back in mind of the conversation he'd had with Fred Gros. His temper rose again and he wished there was something he could do to protect her from the ugliness that folks like that tried to throw at her. Just the thought of someone saying those things, using that tone, to her face had him balling his fists. She might seem tough and unflappable on the outside, but he knew there was a soft, vulnerable place just below that surface that was easily bruised.

He caught her eyeing him curiously and he forcibly relaxed his hands and gave her a smile. "I think we're done. What do you say we call it a night?"

As they exited, Graham dug his keys out of his pocket, but fumbled and dropped them.

"Here, you've got your hands full. Let me get that for you." Reeny picked up the keys and fingered the gold nugget that served as the fob. "Interesting keychain. Looks almost like a piece of jewelry."

Graham's whole being contracted as he fought the urge to

snatch the token from her. It seemed important that nothing about Annie and Reeny intersect.

But almost as if someone else were speaking, he heard himself say, "It was. Once upon a time."

Something in his tone must have given him away. There was a question in her face, but for once she didn't voice it.

Not that her reticence stopped that other voice from continuing. "It used to be a set of wedding bands and an engagement ring."

"Whose?" Her voice was gentle, supportive.

"Mine and my wife's."

"You're married." She quickly corrected herself. "*Were* married."

"Annie died fifteen months ago."

She touched him lightly on the arm, a touch that almost undid him. "Oh Graham, I'm so sorry."

"Me too." Stop talking. His mind practically screamed the command at him. Walk away before you say anything else.

But that part of his mind was no longer in control. "She was pregnant—we'd been trying for so long to have a baby that at the time it seemed like a blessing, an answered prayer. But she developed preeclampsia in her third trimester. Because of Annie's history—she'd had two prior miscarriages—the doctors strongly recommended we abort the pregnancy."

He heard the hitch in her breathing, felt the warmth where her hand still rested on his arm, but the words had been dammed up inside him for too long. Now that they'd finally found a chink, they kept pouring out with unstoppable force. "We both wanted children so badly, both felt so strongly about the sanctity of life, the whole idea of terminating the pregnancy was unthinkable. Besides, we had a veritable army of prayer warriors on our side, and I just knew God wouldn't let anything terrible happen."

He rubbed the back of his neck, wishing that by doing so he could rub away the memories. The anger. The guilt. "She carried our baby almost full-term. But she died on the delivery table. Along with our daughter. So in the end, it was all for nothing."

That's what had hurt so much, that Annie's life had been sacrificed for their child, a child who'd died within minutes of her mother. "So don't talk to me about God, about how faithful He is, about how He answers prayer, about how He never lets you down." He heard his voice escalate in intensity but couldn't get it back under control. "Because I served Him faithfully, I trusted in Him to see us through this. We— I did *everything* right. And He took everything from me."

He saw the pity in her eyes, the understanding and the shimmer of tears not yet released. "Graham, I'm so sorry you went through that. I—" Her voice broke and she lifted her arms, as if to embrace him, and he couldn't take it. Not the pity. Not another perfunctory hug. Not from her.

He turned without another word and headed for his vehicle. He sat there a moment, trying to get his breathing, his pounding pulse, back under control.

He should never have spilled his guts to her like that. The last thing he wanted from Reeny was the same suffocating pity and loss for words he'd left behind in St. Louis.

But there was no turning the clock back. He'd learned that the hard way.

Reeny watched Graham go, her heart breaking at the thought of what he'd endured. The starkness of his words, the raw pain that had emanated from him sliced through her. So much about him was clearer now. *This* was what had created that self-made rift between him and God.

She wrapped her arms around herself, aching for his loss, wishing she could hold him this way. The crushing aloneness of trying to bear it without the solace of turning to God for comfort must have been unbearable.

How had he survived?

Oh Graham, I'm so, so sorry my offer of comfort wasn't enough. Please, don't lock me out, too.

She bowed her head. *Heavenly Father, Graham is hurting and needs You, even if he can't see it right now. Help me to help him find his way back to You again. Because I know it's only through You that one can truly find that promised comfort of the peace that passes all understanding.*

Chapter Eighteen

Graham felt an unaccustomed diffidence as he walked into the practice session Thursday. He hadn't seen Reeny since he'd spilled his guts last Monday. In fact, coward that he was, he'd deliberately avoided her.

How was she going to react?

It wasn't just the pity that had him worried. Had the venom he spewed at God horrified her, made her see him differently? After all, it was one thing to confess he no longer had a close relationship with their Maker, but to rail against Him the way he had must have shocked someone whose beliefs were so obviously deep-rooted.

He mentally braced himself, prepared for a repeat of the smothering sympathy or painfully obvious attempts to ignore the elephant in the room that he'd faced in St. Louis. But a small part of him held on to the hope that with Reeny it would be different....

After an eternity of seconds, she looked up and saw him. The smile that crossed her face was the same unclouded, welcoming smile—with perhaps a trace more warmth—she'd always given him. It was almost as if nothing had passed between them the other night.

Confusion and affront followed on the heels of his relief. How could she *not* view him differently, not have been affected by his story? Surely, after losing a spouse herself, she had to have some idea of the gaping wound it left behind. Or was it just that his pain hadn't made an impact?

Across the room, Ada laughed at something Joscelyn had said. He turned, his gaze latching on to the droll expression on Joscelyn's face as she continued with her story of some ridiculous situation she'd found herself in. Her raspy voice carried to him as if she stood right beside him, and he thought for the first time in a while about what she'd gone through the past few years, how her life had been torn apart and forever changed.

His gaze moved to Dana, the teen who'd lost her parents then found herself whisked away from the comfort of familiar surroundings and friends. He'd warned Reeny about how the girl's issues might affect her interaction with the choir, but had he given much real thought to Dana's pain?

As if he were looking through a shifting tunnel, Andrea caught his attention next. What had it been like for her—giving up her youth to care for an ailing, needy mother?

Were any of their losses, their hurts, less than his? What right did he have to expect Reeny, or anyone else for that matter, to treat his pain as something unique and special? Why did he think God should have made his way any smoother?

Graham immediately pushed that thought away. He had a right to his anger, his—

"Hi, there."

He started, turning to find Reeny at his elbow. When had she crossed the room? How long had he been just standing there?

Her brow puckered. "Sorry, didn't mean to startle you."

He struggled to pull his thoughts together. "No problem. My mind was on something else."

"So I noticed." She gave him a probing look. "Just wanted to let you know I finally convinced Lettie to join us. In fact I think she's actually getting excited about it. She's planning to come to our next practice."

Not the opening he'd expected. "Sounds good. I'll plan to give her some one-on-one time for the next few sessions."

"I knew I could count on you. Lettie takes a little getting used to, but I'm sure y'all will get along fine."

She touched his arm briefly and said softly, "I'm available whenever you want to talk. And I've been praying for you."

Then, before he could respond or even react, she turned and called the group to order.

She was praying for him? He wasn't sure how he felt about that. She wasn't the only one, after all.

However her touch, so gentle, so warm, along with the re-alization that her gaze had held empathy not pity, *did* affect him. It tapped into something deep inside him, so deep that he wasn't sure he even knew what it was, he wasn't sure he dared bring it to the surface.

All through the practice session, he tried to push away his confusion, tried to hold on to his feelings of righteous anger and betrayal, but it was getting harder to do.

He caught Reeny glancing at him a couple of times, concern in her eyes, and tried to focus on his role as assistant choir director. But based on the continued concern he saw shadowing her expression he wasn't doing a very good job of it.

He told himself that the muddled, off-balance feeling would go away before long. Orderly, logical, black and white—that was his way and he'd return to it soon enough. Yep, just as soon as he had time alone to collect himself he'd be okay.

It was a relief when the session finally ended. Rather than spending time in small talk, he went right to work putting away the equipment.

When the last of the choir members had left, Reeny approached him. "Are you feeling all right?"

He had to get away from here, away from *her,* so he could think. If she touched him the way she had before, there was no telling… "I'm fine, just a bit tired. In fact, if you don't mind, I'd like to get things stowed and head home as soon as possible."

"Of course. I can finish up here and lock up if you want to go on."

He was tempted. The less time he spent alone with the perceptive Mrs. Landry right now, the better. But he shook his head. "It's not *that* urgent. Almost done anyway."

Reeny chewed her lip for a moment, worried about the subtle change she saw in Graham. The air of authority and confidence that was so much a part of him seemed to have slipped. She didn't buy his explanation of just being tired.

Was he regretting that he'd told her about the death of his wife? She hoped not. And she needed to tell him that. Whether he wanted to hear it or not.

"About what you told me Monday night…"

He paused midmovement for the merest fraction of time. When he resumed, his whole body was stiff, as if poised for a blow. It hurt to see him like that. "I want you to know I appreciate that you confided in me—I count that a precious gift. I know our situations aren't the same, but I think I understand something of what you're feeling."

That sounded inane, even to her own ears. "Anyway, any time you want to talk, I'm here."

She touched his arm again, trying to transfer a bit of comfort, wishing she could do more. His flinch startled her. Was he rejecting what she offered or was his hurt making him supersensitive?

She forced herself to continue. "Those aren't just words. I mean it." That was what she'd needed most after Ray died—

someone who would just sit by her, perhaps offer a healing touch, and listen while she poured her heart out.

He turned and gave her a polite smile—a smile very reminiscent of the one he'd given her that first day they'd met. "I appreciate the offer." He brushed his hands on his jeans. "Now, I think that's everything. Ready to go?"

Feeling as if she'd somehow failed him, Reeny nodded.

A few minutes later, she started her car and headed for her mother's house.

Heavenly Father, I obviously didn't handle that right, but please, don't let Graham push me away again.

Graham pounded the packed dirt of the jogging trail with more force than usual, making up for lost time. He'd missed his run yesterday—he'd overslept after a late night spent wrestling with unaccustomed doubts and uncomfortable memories.

As he raced along the trail, his jumbled thoughts were replaced with thoughts about Nana. She had a way of cutting through all the pretty wrappings and layers that people tried to surround their actions with and get right to the heart of things.

Sort of the way Reeny did.

Everything in his world seemed to come back around to Reeny these days. He supposed it was because they'd been spending so much time together since he'd first arrived in Tippanyville. Had that really only been a month ago?

At any rate, he'd shaken that off-kilter feeling and had himself back under control now. He'd overreacted Thursday—both in his self-doubts and in his reaction to Reeny's expression of sympathy. Probably his claim of being over-tired had been closer to the truth than he'd realized.

Still, a part of him wondered if he'd made a mistake in not taking her up on her offer. It had actually been cathartic to speak that painful bit of history out loud. Would speaking of it with someone who could understand and empathize—someone like Reeny—make a difference?

Was he brave enough to try?

After yanking the umpteenth weed from the flower bed in front of her house, Reeny sat back on her legs and wiped her forehead with the back of her hand. Then she heard the sound she'd been waiting for—Graham's vehicle turning into his driveway. His Saturday-morning run was finally over. She hadn't seen him since Thursday's practice, but he'd never been far from her mind.

Standing, she tugged off her garden gloves and headed over to talk to him. "Good run?"

He closed the door of his vehicle and stared at her over the hood. "Yep. The mornings are getting cooler, which makes it easier."

She grinned. "By cooler you mean below sweltering."

"Exactly."

She was relieved to see some of the tension she'd sensed Thursday had eased from him. "You seem to be feeling better than the last time I saw you." Was that a flinch? It was there and gone so fast she couldn't be sure.

"Amazing what a couple of good nights' sleep will do for you."

That was a very nice nonanswer. And from where she stood, he didn't look as if he'd been sleeping well at all. But he obviously didn't want to dwell on Thursday evening, or Monday's admission for that matter. So, time to change the subject. "Next Saturday is Desirée's birthday and we're having a little celebration at my house. Nothing fancy—just family and a few friends. Why don't you join us?"

"I wouldn't dream of intruding on a family—"

"Nonsense. It's not just family. Joscelyn, for one, will be

there." Strange, though, how she was beginning to think of him as family. "Besides, Desirée has apparently taken a shine to you. She specifically asked if I would invite you."

She definitely saw something flicker in his eyes at that.

He nodded. "In that case, it sounds like fun."

"Good." Reeny fiddled with the garden gloves she held. "The family-and-friends gathering will start about four o'clock. And feel free to follow your granny's advice about not showing up empty-handed." She grinned. "The love of chocolate in the Perette and Landry households doesn't stop with me and the kids."

He returned her grin, some of that old camaraderie making a reappearance. "You're on."

He hesitated, as if wanting to say something but not sure how to begin. Reeny waited, patiently, hopefully.

Finally he shoved his hands in his pockets. "Reeny, I—"

"Mom." Philip came running out of the house. "Desi spilled maple syrup all over the kitchen floor and Buddy's making a big old mess."

"Oh dear." Reeny bit her lip, glancing back at Graham. "I'm busy right now, Philip. Why don't you shut Buddy in the bathroom and then get out my mop and fill the bucket with water. I'll be in in a few minutes."

Philip looked from her to Graham, a frown on his face.

Graham raked a hand through his hair. "Sounds like you have a minor emergency on your hands. What I had to say'll wait for another day. Go take care of your sticky situation."

She smiled at his pun, but inside she felt like screaming. He'd been about to say something important, she sensed it with every fiber of her being. But the mood was broken and he'd already started toward his porch.

She just prayed that the two of them would have another chance to have that conversation.

Chapter Nineteen

Graham crossed over to Reeny's carport, Desirée's gift in hand. Things between him and Reeny had settled back into their familiar routine. Their after-practice discussion sessions were as comfortable as ever, and with Lettie joining them this week, they'd had a lot to discuss.

He could tell Reeny was waiting for him to finish that conversation he'd started in his driveway last week, but she didn't push. To be honest, he wasn't even sure himself what he'd been about to say.

His knock on Reeny's door was greeted with an "It's open, come on in" hail. He stepped inside to find her working at the kitchen counter.

"Oh, hi," she said. "Everyone's out back on the patio. I'm just refilling the chip bowl and getting more ice."

"Here, let me help." He set the gift on the counter and took the ice bucket from her.

She eyed the wrapped package. "You didn't have to bring a gift."

"What sort of cad would go to a little girl's birthday party empty-handed?"

She laughed. "Come on, I'll introduce you to my brother."

Graham followed her outside to discover that indeed everyone was already there. Her mother and in-laws were seated around a table next to the grill, Joscelyn was pushing Desirée on the tree swing and Philip was tossing a football with a fellow who had to be Reeny's brother.

She set the bowl of chips down and moved to the edge of the patio. "Hey, Jake, come over here for a minute."

"Coming." Reeny's brother threw a spiraling pass to Philip, then trotted over to them, putting a hand over Reeny's shoulder.

She bumped him with her hip, then turned to Graham. "Graham, this is my big brother, Jake Perette. Jake, this is my new next-door neighbor, Graham Lockwood."

As they shook hands, Graham could feel himself being sized up and he returned the favor.

Jake finally stepped past him to retrieve a glass of iced tea from the table. "Reeny tells me you've been a big help with this handbell choir of hers."

From the corner of his eye, Graham saw Lavinia stiffen. Did Jake not know about the rift?

"She's doing most of the work," he said. "I'm just lending a hand where needed." Then he quickly changed the subject. "So, what kind of law practice do you have?"

"Civil matters mostly. I—"

"Uncle Jake." Philip's voice carried from across the yard. "Aren't you going to come throw the ball some more?"

"Sure enough, sport." He turned back to Reeny. "You up for a game of touch?"

"Oh, I don't know, Jake. I—"

"Don't tell me you're getting soft in your old age, sis." He crossed his arms, a note of challenge in his expression. "Or are you afraid to let your new neighbor see me whoop you."

Her eyes narrowed. "You're on. And Mr. Sits-in-an-office-all-day, we'll see just who whoops who."

In a matter of a few minutes Graham found himself in the midst of a family-style touch football game. Desirée, as the birthday girl, divided them up into teams. She pitted Graham, Reeny and herself against Jake, Joscelyn and Philip. The older adults declined to play, instead they alternately served as cheerleaders and as referees from the shaded comfort of the patio.

About twenty minutes into the game, with the score tied, Reeny tripped and fell as she tried to tag Philip.

Graham got to her first, his pulse kicking up a notch when she didn't pop right back up. "Are you okay?" He took her hand, studying her for signs of injury.

"I think so." She sat up, pulling a leaf from her hair. "Just knocked the wind out of me."

He frowned as he noticed a raw spot on her arm. "You're bleeding."

"Oh." She stared at it as if just now noticing. "It's only a little scrape. No need to make a fuss."

When she tried to stand, Graham put a hand at the small of her back and one at her good elbow to assist. He wasn't taking any chances. "All the same, I think you should take care of it right away."

"The man's right." Joscelyn turned to Graham. "Why don't you help her into the house so she can tend to it?"

"But what about our game?" Philip's tone made it clear he wanted to continue.

"I think the game's over, sport." Jake tossed him the ball. "Let's see if your Pa-paw needs help getting the meat on the grill."

Graham slowly led Reeny inside, keeping an arm protectively around her waist as he did so. The fact that she leaned against him, favoring her right leg ever so slightly, felt less of a burden than a privilege. Her arm at his back felt delightfully warm, her hair tickled his nose playfully and her vanilla scent wrapped around him in an embrace of its own.

Nope, this was no hardship at all.

Reeny allowed Graham to seat her at the kitchen table and gave him instructions on where to find the bandages, antibiotic and a clean rag. It was hard to gather her thoughts any further than that. That look of worry and concern Graham had given her, the gentle, almost possessive way he'd held her hand and then helped her up, had sent little tingles down her spine.

Then when he put his arm around her to help her into the house, her mind had slipped into a delicious confusion. The security of his hold, the warmth of his touch, the attitude of protectiveness with maybe just a hint of possessiveness had set her senses spinning.

But was he feeling the same thing? Was there real caring there, something that went beyond friendship? Or was she only seeing what she wanted to see?

"Reeny."

She realized he was back at her side, a damp rag in one hand, the first-aid items in his other.

"Yes?"

"I'm going to wash the scrape now. Let me know if I hurt you."

She hid a grin. Really, it was only a little scratch. But she was enjoying this attention too much to protest.

The care he took with her hurt was every bit as gentle and endearing as she'd expected. When he had her bandaged to his satisfaction, he frowned down at her leg. "You were limping when we crossed the yard. Is it your ankle?"

"It hurt a little earlier but it wasn't anything. It's all better now."

He studied her face as if he suspected her of lying. "Are you sure?"

Oh, he really was sweet. "One hundred percent. Thanks for the ointment and the bandage—I'm good as new." She stood up and took a few steps to prove her point.

And all the time her waist remembered the touch of his arm, her elbow tingled where he'd so gently tended to her.

What was happening to her?

Once Graham was certain Reeny was really okay, he returned outside. Rather than joining the others, though, he offered to push Desirée on the swing. He needed some time to think, to process what had just happened.

The overwhelming, heart-pounding urge to protect and comfort Reeny when he'd seen her fall had taken him completely by surprise. He'd latched on to her hand and hadn't wanted to release her until he was absolutely certain she was okay.

The only other person he'd ever felt that way about was Annie. How could he betray her by falling in love with someone else?

How could he risk the gut-wrenching, soul-wrenching pain of possibly losing that beloved one again.

He couldn't.

He swallowed a groan, fearing it was already too late.

Her mom and brother were the last to leave that evening. Jake gave her a brotherly one-armed hug as they waited by the front door for their mom to say a last good-night to Philip and Desirée. "I'm staying at Mom's tonight," he said, "so I'll see the three of y'all at church tomorrow."

"Good. There's quite a few folk who've been asking after you, so you can catch them all up on the latest."

"Mr. Popular, that's me."

She grinned at his posturing. "More like the prodigal son."

"Ah, sis, your jealousy of me is *so* not attractive." Then he turned serious. "This Graham, he seems like an okay guy."

Had she been so obvious that he felt the need to give his big-brother stamp of approval? "He is."

"Seems to get along well with the kids, too."

"That he does." She gave him a don't-you-dare-take-this-any-further look.

But he seemed oblivious. "I just wanted—"

"Sorry to keep you waiting." Their mother bustled into the room, rescuing Reeny from having to endure more of her brother's heavy-handed comments.

Estelle grabbed her purse and joined them at the door. "Now are you sure you don't need any more help with the cleanup?"

"You've done more than enough, Mom. Besides, the only thing left to do is take out the trash."

"Jake, why don't you—"

"Mom, I'm perfectly capable of carrying a trash bag from the kitchen to the carport." She made shooing motions. "Ya'll just run on and have some nice mother-son time."

Once they'd gone, Reeny gathered up the last of the crumpled napkins from the party and stuffed them into a nearly full trash bag. It had been a very busy day but she wasn't tired.

Desirée had loved being the center of attention, and both of the kids adored their uncle Jake. And even Ray's mom had called a truce for the day.

Graham seemed to fit right in. He and Jake had gotten along well—just as she'd suspected they would. It was almost as if he were part of the family….

This time she didn't push the thought away. Instead she allowed it to roll around in her mind. She was ready to admit that perhaps she felt something a little stronger than friendship for Graham. And surprisingly, the guilt she'd expected to feel at that admission wasn't there. Instead there was a sense of peace, of rightness.

Ray, you know you were my first love. You're the only guy I ever so much as kissed. And your memory will always bring me joy. But I think I'm finally ready to move on.

Because I love Graham, scarred heart and all.

She tied off the trash bag then stepped outside and dumped it into the large garbage can she kept under the carport. She made sure the lid was on tight then dusted off her hands. Before she could head back inside, however, she saw Graham's carport light switch on. A moment later he stepped outside and opened the door of his vehicle. Was he going somewhere?

But no, it looked as if he was just retrieving something.

She hadn't turned her own light on so he probably hadn't noticed her. She started to call out a greeting, then paused. Given her thoughts a few moments ago, she felt suddenly shy, uncertain how to act around him. After all, just because she felt this way, didn't mean he returned the feeling or would even welcome knowing how she felt.

Then he glanced over and took the choice out of her hands.

"Hello, neighbor." He strolled closer. "Thanks again for inviting me over today. I enjoyed myself."

"I'm glad you came. And Desirée loves the origami kit you gave her. That was such a thoughtful gesture."

"Glad she likes it."

Reeny felt her pulse kick up a notch in reaction to his nearness and searched for something to say. "Jake is spending the night at Mom's and plans to attend services in the morning. The invitation is still open if you want to join us. I know you said—"

He touched a finger to her lips to stop her words. "Don't. I'm not ready for that yet."

His touch—warm, firm, gentle—left her breathless. Did he feel it, too? Or was it just friendship to him? Did his love for his deceased wife still run too strong to allow him to commit to another?

His finger moved to stroke the skin just above the corner of her mouth. "A little smudge of chocolate…"

A pulse jumped right where his finger stroked. He'd felt

her reaction—she could tell by the way his finger stilled, the way his gaze locked on hers. She searched his face, looking for answers, and saw the reflection of her own emotions in his eyes. She rested a hand against his chest and felt the hammering of his heart.

His finger moved again, skimming down her face until it rested under her chin.

His eyes searched hers more intently, as if seeking permission. If that's what he sought, he found it. His face lowered and she lifted hers, eager for the promised kiss.

The sound of the screen door screeching open broke the spell and Reeny pulled back like a guilty teenager. She spun around to find her son standing in the doorway, a shocked look on his face.

"Mom!" Philip's voice was thick with indignation and disapproval.

Reeny brushed at her shoulder, trying to regain her dignity. "What is it, Philip?"

"What are you doing out here with Mr. Lockwood?"

Reeny winced at her son's not-very-subtle question. "That's neither here nor there. I assume you need something since you're out of bed and it's past ten o'clock."

Graham cleared his throat. "I'll head back to my place. Thanks again for an enjoyable evening."

Reeny fought the urge to call him back, instead moving to the door. She ushered her son back into the kitchen ahead of her. "I'll ask again. What are you doing up?"

But Philip wouldn't be distracted. "You were going to kiss him, weren't you?" He said it as if she'd been contemplating highway robbery.

"Look, Philip, I know you loved your dad, and I loved him very much, too—still do. But he's gone now and—"

"But you can't date Mr. Lockwood—he's my *math teacher*. It's just not right."

Ah, so it was a peer-pressure thing. "He won't be your math teacher forever, son. And I know you like Mr. Lockwood. Why you—"

"I hate that old handbell choir. You should've done like Ma-maw said and built a bridge in the park, then none of this would have happened."

His words sliced at her like a dagger. "You don't mean that. Think of all the fun we've had these past few weeks."

"I don't care." And with that he turned and ran back to his room, slamming the door behind him.

What in the world had she done?

Graham lay in bed and stared up at the ceiling, unable to sleep. No matter how good, how right it felt, touching her lips had been a very bad idea. Kissing Reeny Landry would have been an even worse idea, no matter how much he'd wanted to do it, no matter what his feelings for her.

Look what *almost* kissing her had accomplished. He'd given her the impression that theirs was a relationship that could go somewhere. And he'd antagonized her son, one of his students, in the process.

Besides, if she had it in her head that she'd be the one to ease him back into a revival of faith, she was sadly mistaken.

Better if he took a few steps back, tried to return their relationship to its former easy friendship status. He'd done it once. He could do it again.

Couldn't he?

Chapter Twenty

Reeny pushed away the checkbook register for The Petal Pusher Flower Shop. She'd promised Wilma she'd have everything balanced, entered in the computer and back to her by the end of the week. But she'd been staring at the same column of figures for thirty minutes now and not making any progress.

Just a week and a half ago she'd felt on top of the world. Today she had trouble summoning a genuine smile.

Philip had been sullen and uncommunicative ever since the night of Desirée's party. Jake had picked up on the something's-wrong-here signal almost immediately on Sunday morning, but thankfully Philip hadn't said anything about what had set him off. Probably too embarrassed by his mother's actions.

Graham, who she'd only seen at the three practice sessions since that night, had been oh so pleasant and excruciatingly polite, but there'd been no more of those warm glances and shared smiles. And he'd blocked her two attempts to talk about what had happened that night.

Did Philip's approval mean so much to him? Or did her feelings mean so little?

Then again, maybe he just regretted the whole thing. Had his almost kiss been merely a reaction to something he saw in her expression under the darkened carport, some need she hadn't been able to disguise?

That was just too mortifying a scenario to contemplate.

As if all of that wasn't bad enough, Graham's and Philip's moods—and to be honest hers, as well—seemed to be rubbing off on the rest of the choir. There'd been a tension in the air these last three sessions that hadn't been there before. And the little spark of attraction that she'd watched build between Dana and Mark had apparently turned sour.

It had all come to a head this past Monday. They'd arrived at the practice hall to find the air conditioner had gone on the fritz. Add stifling heat to already edgy nerves and it had not been a pleasant session. Tempers had been short, everyone's timing seemed to be off and no one had stayed around to chat after the session ended.

Thank goodness the repairman she'd called had been able to fix it yesterday. She'd been poised to call off tonight's practice if he hadn't. Even so, she needed to get her own attitude in order before she could hope to tease back the choir's earlier joy in their fellowship.

Reeny put her pen down and went to the kitchen for a fresh cup of coffee. To top everything else off, there was the whole issue of the Bayou Cigale footbridge. Lately there'd been some renewed talk about needing to replace it, and she'd caught more than one censoring look shot her way whenever the subject came up.

It made it hard to remember that replacing that bridge had never been her responsibility in the first place.

She glanced at the clock. Two hours left before it would be time to pick up the kids from school. She'd better make the most of them. Taking her coffee with her, she headed back to her office. The sound of the fire truck's siren caught her attention and she paused to say a quick prayer for Jeff and the other firemen, as well as for whoever might be in the fire's path.

Just as she set her coffee mug down on her desk, the phone rang. A quick glance at the caller ID display indicated it was coming from Lettie's beauty shop.

Puzzled, she placed the phone at her ear. "Hello."

"Reeny, it's Lettie. You need to head over to the practice hall right away. There's been a fire."

Nobody was hurt.
Nobody was hurt.

Reeny kept repeating that in her head as if it were a mantra.

She would worry about what this meant for the handbell choir later. For today, she would give thanks for that very precious blessing.

She faced the charred shell of what had been their practice hall. Her mother stood on one side of her and Graham stood on the other. Both of them had hold of one of her hands. She was grateful to have their strength to draw on.

Jeff, covered in soot and attired in his fireman's gear, walked up, carrying the sign Andrea had carved for them all those weeks ago. It now seemed a lifetime ago.

"Mrs. Landry, I'm so sorry, but we weren't able to save much. Just this."

Nodding, she freed her hands, immediately missing the warmth and security of Graham's touch. As if he'd read her mind, Graham's hand moved to her shoulder just as she accepted the unwieldy sign. Hugging the sign against her chest, she closed her eyes, taking a second to savor that much-needed connection with Graham. She inhaled deeply and looked around. It seemed most of the town was gathered around. Sure, she knew some of them were here just to gawk, but most wore sympathetic expressions.

Her mind flitted from one detail to the next, taking in the trivial with the significant, able to stay focused on nothing.

Lavinia stood several feet away, a stricken expression on her face.

Wilma, still clutching a bunch of daisies, was talking to the fire chief.

Most of the choir members—her precious Ding-a-lings—stood together. Only Philip and Desirée were absent.

How had Mark and Dana gotten out of school? Had they been excused or had they slipped away?

Not that that mattered right now. What mattered was that all of them wore shocked, lost expressions. And they were staring at her, looking for some kind of answer, some kind of where-do-we-go-from-here guidance.

She wanted to protest, to tell them that she didn't have the answers and that she needed reassurances as much as they did.

Then she pushed that selfish thought away. She was their director and their friend. No, she didn't have the answers, but she knew who did. She squared her shoulders and let her gaze meet Graham's briefly.

"Give it here." He gently took the sign from her, handed it to Mark, and this time took one of her hands while he put the other around her shoulder. She wanted to just melt into him, but she took courage instead from the knowledge that he was there to hold her up for as long as she needed him.

He'd said so.

Thank You Lord, for bringing Graham into my life. Whether he wants to be just friends, or something deeper, my world is the richer for having him in it.

"I'd like to offer up a prayer right now." She pitched her voice loud enough for everyone to hear. "Any of you who have a mind to join me can draw near and find someone's hand to hold."

As the crowd shuffled closer, she felt Graham tighten his hold on her hand. His gaze held hers a moment, sending waves of concern, support and approval washing through her. Then he squeezed her hand again and bowed his head.

His actions almost undid her. That he would offer her the comfort of his prayers, when he had suffered such a tremendous crisis of faith, was unbelievably touching. If God had used this disaster to accomplish nothing else but to begin the thaw of Graham's relationship with Him, then she could be content.

She drew a deep breath and bowed her head. "Heavenly Father, we come to you in thanksgiving that no one was hurt and that no other business suffered damage in this fire. We know it could have been so much worse and are grateful that Your hedge of protection was around us this day. We rest in the assurance that through this seemingly awful occurrence, You will find a way to work Your will for us, whether we recognize Your hand in that outcome or not."

She paused a moment, gathering her thoughts. "Help us in the days to come as we deal with picking up the pieces to remember Your grace to us this day. And help us to remember, too, that no matter the circumstances, with You standing beside us, we can boldly claim, it is well with my soul."

Graham listened to her words, her voice shaky at first but growing steadier and stronger as she prayed. Despite what he knew had to be a major blow to her hopes and dreams for this ministry, it appeared her faith was as solid as ever.

Her final words humbled him, almost driving him to his knees. Not only was her faith unshaken, but she was looking for ways to find good in the midst of this.

Unbidden, the memory of a long-ago conversation with Nana popped into his head. It was the year he turned thirteen. While most of his friends were enjoying their summer vacation, he'd slaved away cutting lawns and taking whatever other odd jobs he could find, saving his earnings to buy a new bike he had his eye on.

When the big day came, he'd ridden into town with Granddad, impatiently accompanying him on his other errands, before they finally pulled up at the bicycle store. But when it came time to pay for the bike, he discovered his money was gone. They searched the truck, retraced all their steps, but it was nowhere. Whether the money had fallen out of his pocket or a thief had lifted it, the money was long gone.

When they returned home, he'd groused and complained and grumbled about the unfairness of it all and about just what should be done to whoever had ended up with his money. Finally Nana had had enough and told him to stop complaining and have faith that God was somehow going to use the situation to do good—if not for him then for someone who needed either the money or the lesson more.

When he'd mumbled some smart-alecky remark under his breath about rather having the money than faith, Nana had immediately sat him down and given him one of her I'm-very-disappointed-in-you looks.

"True faith is the only thing in this life that can get you through the hard times," she'd said. "But faith isn't faith if it's not tested. It's just gratitude. That's nothing special—even that old stray dog that comes around here looking for scraps can show gratitude. But when blessings don't come, or if they get taken away, now that's when the true test of a body's faith comes in."

He thought he'd understood what she meant back then, but he was beginning to believe he'd forgotten the heart of it somewhere along the way.

But Reeny had grasped its essence with both hands. How had she found the strength?

A few minutes later the crowd began to disperse. Reeny

continued to stand there, as if not sure where to go. Worried about her, Graham led her to his vehicle, stopping briefly to say something to her mother.

He stood next to her as she climbed in and buckled up, then shut the door and went around to his side. She didn't say a word until he pulled into his driveway.

"I left my car back there."

"Your mother is going to take care of it. And she's going to pick up the kids at school and take care of them for a few hours, too. For now you are to let me take care of you. Understood?"

Reeny stared at him for a long moment, then her lips quirked up in a smile. "Aye, aye, Captain."

That was better. "Come on, I'm going to cook you an omelet."

She obediently followed him up the stairs to his front door. "But it's not suppertime."

"A little nourishment would likely do us both good right now. And then I'm thinking a rousing game of checkers."

She gave him a surprised look. "Checkers? I haven't played that since I was a kid."

"Then it's about time you played again."

By the third game of checkers, which she won, Graham was satisfied that she would be all right. The bruised look was gone from her eyes and some of the tension had left her, as well. She was even laughing at his occasional attempts at humor.

Funny how she caught on to his subtle sense of the absurd so much quicker than folks who'd known him for years.

A little later he drove her to her mom's to pick up her kids and her car, and came around to open the door for her. "Give me a call when you get ready to start laying interim plans for the choir. We can brainstorm together."

Reeny smiled up at him. "I will." Then she placed her hand

on his arm. "Thank you so much for this afternoon. It's been a very long time since I've had someone pamper me the way you did. It meant a lot."

The soft look in her eyes was so sweet, so melting, he almost grabbed her up in his arms and promised to give her as many of those afternoons as she wanted. Instead he touched her cheek. "It was my pleasure."

Her eyes darkened, and he saw a shiver flutter through her. Then she was gone, hurrying up the walkway to her mother's house without a backward glance.

He wasn't sure how much more of this self-inflicted torture he could stand.

Chapter Twenty-One

Reeny sat at her kitchen table, sipping on her first cup of coffee of the day, a pencil in her hand and a pad of paper in front of her. It was Saturday morning and, after all the upheaval of the past day and a half, she was letting the kids sleep late, so it was just her and Buddy.

The faint wail of a siren raised Buddy's head from the floor and Reeny shuddered as the memories of Thursday's fire came flooding back. After saying a quick prayer for whoever that emergency vehicle was being dispatched for, she returned to her coffee.

Yesterday she'd felt under the weather, a reaction no doubt to all the stress. The all-day and all-night downpour hadn't helped any, either. But she'd had the memory of that afternoon of being pampered by Graham to cheer her up.

Her lips curled up in a smile at the thought of Graham. He'd been amazingly supportive since the fire.

Not only had he given her that lovely afternoon Thursday, but yesterday he'd stopped by twice, once in the morning before school to share a cup of coffee, and then last night he'd joined them for movie night.

Remarkably, Philip had been sobered enough by what happened that he hadn't raised a fuss.

Graham had done most of the talking, touching on topics from the ridiculous to the sublime, but he'd done more than that. He'd been there with a quick reassuring touch, seeming to understand exactly when she needed the connection. He'd spoken matter-of-factly of the choir's next practice session as if there was no doubt in his mind that it would continue. And he'd never once asked her inane questions about how she was feeling.

Best of all, he'd sat and listened after the movie last night when she wanted to talk. She couldn't even remember what all she'd said. She just remembered the comforting feel of his presence as he let her unload boatloads of pent-up emotion and frustration, some of which, she suspected, had absolutely nothing to do with the fire.

A part of her knew this was temporary, that soon, when he thought she'd had time to recover, Graham would step back and Philip would get surly again. But for now she wanted to savor it and pretend it was leading up to something very nice.

Buddy's bark alerted her that she had a visitor before she ever heard the knock. She opened the door to see Graham standing there, his hand raised to knock again, a look of concern on his face.

Had he stopped by to check on her again?

She unlatched the screen door with a smile. "Come on in. I was just—"

"I see you haven't heard."

The mix of grim relief and somber demeanor sent a frisson of worry up her spine. "Heard what? Has something else happened at the hall?"

"No." He raked his hand through his hair, his grim expression deepening. "I just came from my jog at the park. There's been an accident."

Reeny moved back to the table and plopped down in her chair. She wasn't sure how much more bad news she could take. "What kind of accident?" *Please God, don't let anyone be hurt.*

"Grady Richard and his grandson, Ben, were fishing off the bridge. One of the supports shifted and Ben fell in."

Her heart constricted. Ben was only four years old. "Is he all right?"

"He took a pretty hard lick to his head and got water in his lungs, but the EMTs think he's going to be okay. They've taken him by ambulance to the hospital just to be sure."

"Grady must be beside himself. And Linda and Tom— Ben's their only child. Oh." A chill gripped her as she took in the rest of it. The bridge—

"Reeny, look at me." He placed a hand on each shoulder and squeezed lightly. "Look at me. This is not your fault."

The very act of him saying that out loud felt like a conviction. "If only I'd given the money to the town like everyone wanted this would never—"

Looking at her stricken expression, Graham tried again to get through to her. "I said, this is *not* your fault." But he saw the dullness of defeat still clouding her eyes, the crushing weight of a guilt that wasn't hers bowing her shoulders.

He'd known she'd take it hard, that she'd blame herself— that's why he'd rushed over as soon as he realized what had happened. She deserved to get the news from someone who would understand and cared about her reaction.

And he did care. More than just a little.

He waited for the guilt and push back that should have accompanied that admission, but none came. When had this sense of rightness, of meant-to-be, crept into his feelings for her?

He gave his head a mental shake, focusing back on Reeny. Time enough to mull over his epiphany later.

He glanced at her half-empty cup. "Have you had anything for breakfast besides that paint stripper you call coffee?"

His weak joke about the chicory brew earned him a half smile.

"No. I was planning to fix a bowl of cereal when—"

"I don't think a cold breakfast will cut it this morning. What you need is one of my sweep-the-kitchen omelets."

"There's no need—"

"I'll be afraid you didn't like my other omelet if you refuse." He moved to the door. "Get out your largest skillet while I'm gone—I plan to make enough for the kids, too. Give me ten minutes to clean up and gather ingredients, and I'll be right back." Not giving her time to make additional excuses, he quickly made his exit.

It had become his personal mission to have her smile make it all the way back to her eyes.

After breakfast Reeny shooed him away, insisting she was fine and that she had a busy day ahead of her.

He didn't believe her on the first point and worried about what she planned to do with the second, but he reluctantly complied. He understood she needed a little space to figure things out. But by one o'clock, he figured he'd given her enough time on her own.

When she answered his knock, all he could read in her expression was composure. "Come on in," she said as she stepped back. "I was just fixing to take a pitcher of lemonade out back to share with the kids."

He wasn't sure if that was an invitation or a polite way of saying she didn't have time for him. He decided to go with the first. "Mind if I join you?"

Did he imagine the slight hesitation?

"Not at all. Grab an extra glass and come on out."

By the time Graham followed her out, she was already

pouring up the citrus drink for her two very thirsty-looking kids. Desirée greeted him with her normal unfettered exuberance. Philip, while not exactly overjoyed to see him, had put aside his outright hostility for the time being. The boy obviously sensed his mother was going through a tough time and was concerned for her enough not to exacerbate the situation.

Once the children had moved back into the yard to play, Graham took a seat on one of the patio chairs next to Reeny. "I checked in on Ben. He's going to be fine. They're keeping him overnight just for observation, but expect to send him home tomorrow."

She nodded. "Mom called to tell me. Praise God. I know the family must be heaving a sigh of relief."

He couldn't quite put his finger on what, but something in her voice, in the way she held herself, seemed slightly off. "I talked to Wilma, too." He watched her closely. "She plans to take the insurance money and rebuild. She also wants to talk to you about any input you want to have into the floor plan."

Reeny traced a droplet of water sliding down her glass. "Tell her not to rebuild on my account."

He definitely didn't like the sound of that. "What do you mean?"

She drew her legs up and hugged her knees, still not meeting his gaze. "It's taken me a while but I've finally gotten the message. This handbell choir was a mistake, a selfish dream. I should have listened to wiser counsel."

"There was nothing selfish about your dream. And wasn't it God's counsel you sought?"

She eyed him curiously, as if surprised by his mention of God. "Yes, but that doesn't mean I didn't misinterpret his answer."

She stared out over the yard. "It's probably served its purpose anyway. Carrie has moved on to start over elsewhere. I can get Desirée piano lessons, so she can continue to explore musical expression. Dana wasn't that interested to start with, so she shouldn't really be upset if it goes away. Mark can still put it on his college transcript. Andrea has come out of her shell a lot and I think she'll be able to find other ways to connect. Lettie doesn't have much time invested right now so I don't think she'll really miss it. Ada, Clotile and Mom will move on to other projects. Jeff can feel like he's repaid his debt to Ray."

She smiled grimly. "Everybody's happy."

She'd obviously put a lot of thought into this since breakfast. He shouldn't have left her alone so long. "What about Geralyn? And Joscelyn?"

Reeny winced, but refused to be swayed. "They're both strong women. They'll be fine."

"And all the work everyone's put into getting ready for the Fall Festival? Isn't that a commitment we need to live up to?"

"Of course. Edith has helped me locate some loaner bells we can use for practice and for the performance. I plan to drive up to Alexandria Monday to pick them up.

"Mt. Calvary has agreed to let us use the choir room to hold our practice sessions and to store our equipment. They have tables we can borrow, but I still need to purchase foam pads."

She let her legs down and shifted forward as if to reach for her notebook. Instead, she leaned back again. "I reordered the music, but it won't be in until Tuesday so we'll need to move Monday's practice back one day this week."

She'd been busy. And naturally she'd done it without asking for help. "I'll take care of the foam pads," Graham offered.

She cut him a quick glance and he thought for a moment she would protest. Then she nodded. "If you wish. I don't plan to permanently re-equip the choir. I'm going to take the insurance money and donate it to the town's Bayou Cigale Footbridge Replacement Fund. I also plan to get involved in the project so I can make certain we have a structure that's as safe as we can make it."

He couldn't believe she was giving up. What had happened to that strong woman of faith who saw every setback as testing, every success as the touch of God's hand? "Reeny, no matter what anyone tried to tell you, replacing that bridge was not your responsibility. What *happened* was not your fault. They're saying now that all the rain this past week washed out the bank beneath the supports."

Reeny looked at him, her vulnerability almost hidden behind the hardness of her expression. "In other words, an act of God."

She couldn't seriously believe she was culpable. "That's not—"

She held up a hand. "I appreciate what you're trying to do. But you can say whatever you want, it still won't change how I feel. Besides, now Philip will be happy and you can go back to focusing on being a schoolteacher. Just like you wanted."

He winced, knowing he deserved that. "What time do we leave on Monday?"

She frowned. "I can handle it. Don't you have to teach?"

"I'll take a personal day. And you'll need my SUV." There was no way he was going to let her make that drive alone.

She looked as if she would argue further, but then shrugged. "Nine o'clock. That'll give me time to be back before the kids get out of school."

He hated seeing her like this, as if all the fight had gone out of her. She looked tired and defeated and lost. The urge to comfort her, to wrap his arms around her, to offer his chest to rest her head against was strong.

But he didn't have that right. And the last time he'd come even close to something like that had ended in disaster.

But someday very soon…

Chapter Twenty-Two

The drive to Alexandria was strikingly different from the last road trip they'd taken together. Rather than the bouncy excitement and let's-get-to-know-each-other conversations she'd bubbled over with last time, today she was quiet and controlled. The conversation was listless, lacked eye contact and was mostly one-sided.

By the time they were loaded up and headed back to Tippanyville, Graham had grown desperate to shake her up. "Have you told everyone yet about your plans?"

She shook her head. "I called them all to let them know I'd located equipment and that we'd be practicing at Mt. Calvary, but not the rest. I'll make the announcement at practice." She didn't meet his gaze. "I thought they deserved to hear it face-to-face."

At least the caring-about-people part of her was still intact.

When they arrived at the church, Reeny's pastor was there to greet them. He took Reeny's hands in his. "I was so sorry to hear about the fire. I know it's hard to see something you worked so hard at literally go up in flames."

"Thank you. And I appreciate the church allowing us to make use of the choir room."

Then she turned to Graham. "Have you two met?"

Graham stepped forward. "I don't believe I've had the honor." He held out his hand. "Graham Lockwood."

"David Larrimer."

The two men shook hands, then the preacher followed them around to the back of the vehicle. "Here, let me help."

Once everything was stored away, the pastor handed Reeny a key. "Since you're a church member, the Property Committee voted to let you have a key to the building. Be sure to let us know if there's anything else we can do for you."

"Thank you. We appreciate all of the kindness you extended."

The pastor nodded. "Your group is more than welcome to stay here for however long it takes to get your other facility up and running again."

Graham saw the flicker of regret in her expression, but she merely nodded and said another thank-you before heading for the exit. So, she wasn't yet ready to verbalize her decision.

Perhaps he could snap her out of this miasma she'd fallen into yet. It was important to him for more than one reason.

He'd finally reconciled his feelings for Annie with his feelings for Reeny. Loving one didn't preclude loving the other. And opening himself up to pain was a moot point. He already loved her, already hurt for her.

Trouble was, he knew with absolute certainty that if he told her his feelings now she wouldn't believe him. She was so turned around over this guilt thing that she was pushing everyone away. She would convince herself he was just being kind.

When he declared himself, he wanted her thinking straight and unencumbered by reasons to doubt. He'd wait as long as it took.

He just hoped it didn't take too long….

* * *

Reeny's mind was made up. It was truly kind of Graham to try to make her feel better—he'd gone above and beyond these past few days—but she'd finally seen the light.

It had been one thing to stand against her mother-in-law and the others when she'd felt she was doing the right thing, but now she no longer held that conviction.

Ray's mom had been right. Or maybe they both had. Maybe she was supposed to get this group together for a while, give these people the taste of the kind of fellowship they could find if they put forth the effort and then set them loose so the money could be turned to more general use. She drew some comfort from that thought. After all, while everyone had gotten a big scare out of Ben's accident, no one had been seriously hurt.

Yet.

Graham had spent the better part of yesterday and this afternoon, trying to convince her to hold off making her announcement.

"At least wait until after the Fall Festival," he'd argued.

"And just what purpose would that serve?"

"If you tell them now it's going to take the wind right out of their sails. How do you expect them to give their all to this performance if they know it all ends the next day? Let them enjoy this one achievement before you pull the rug out from under them."

She hadn't liked his choice of words but had tried not to let the sting show. "Holding back would feel like lying."

He'd given her a challenging glare. "And what's more important here—your feelings or theirs."

Miss Ada and Miss Clotile had arrived before she could respond, and that's how they'd left it.

She had to admit, though, standing in front of the group now, it was hard summoning up the right words. Finally she cleared her throat. "Good evening, everyone. I'm glad the schedule switch didn't stop any of you from coming."

"Couldn't wait to get back to it," Miss Ada called out.

"That's right," Joscelyn added. "And don't you worry, we'll make up for that lost session in no time."

Additional supportive comments came from several members, catching Reeny off guard. This was going to be much harder than she'd imagined.

"I've already talked to the Glory Be's," Clotile said. "Everyone's agreed to help make nice new cloths for our tables to replace the old ones—in fact we've already started. So don't you go spending money on new ones."

Dana spoke up next. "My grandma says she's going to rebuild the practice hall with the insurance money. If the builders can get started right away, we might even be able to move in before Christmas."

While the group was clapping over the good news, Reeny caught Graham's knowing glance and quickly looked away. Just because something was difficult didn't mean it shouldn't be done. "Thank you all. Before we get started, I have an announcement to make." Start easy. "These handbells we're using are on loan from the Fellowship Church of Alexandria. They've made them available until after the Fall Festival."

She paused, drawing courage for the bombshell announcement. And suddenly she couldn't do it. Graham was right. The spirit in the room right now was higher and sweeter than it had ever been and it would be cruel to deflate that, especially after the emotional drain and stress of the fire. Better to wait until after the performance. What could another two weeks hurt?

Graham stopped by Joscelyn's office Wednesday morning. "Got a minute?"

"Sure, what's up?"

"I need to talk to someone who knows Reeny better than I do."

Joscelyn raised a brow. "And by better, I assume you mean longer. 'Cause I think you have a pretty good handle on her already."

"She's thinking about abandoning the handbell choir."

Joscelyn's smile faded. "The accident on the footbridge."

It was a statement, not a question. She'd leaped right past the obvious conclusion that the fire had done this and hit the mark. "Yep. She's finally accepted that all the naysayers were right and she should have spent the money there."

"That girl can be so hardheaded. I've told her time and again that being so willing to accept responsibility is *not* a virtue—she needs to give God a chance to work in other people's lives, too." Joscelyn leaned back in her chair. "So what are we gonna do about it?"

Graham smiled, glad to have found an ally. "This is where I need your help…."

Chapter Twenty-Three

The morning of the Fall Festival, Reeny donned her uniform. It would all be over soon. She was going to miss the choir, but it was really for the best.

But if that was true, why was her heart so heavy?

She was so proud of all they'd accomplished. She knew in her heart they were ready for this performance.

Not only that, but the way they had all come together had been amazing and heart-warming. Jeff had brought in a set of small wooden tabletop stands to prop up the plain binders they were currently using. He'd been embarrassed by everyone's oohs and aahs, saying a lot of the credit should go to his fellow firemen. They'd apparently helped construct the stands from scrap lumber because, as Mark put it, they were always looking for a project like this to help pass the time.

Shy Andrea had taken it upon herself to get permission from Mt. Calvary's choir director to put a couple of hooks in the wall so they could hang their Ding-a-ling sign whenever practice was in session.

Her mom, Miss Ada and Miss Clotile had brought in the promised table cloths from the Glory Be's. They were made of a green fabric similar to the curtains Miss Ada had made for their former headquarters and, like the curtains, they had the gold appliquéd handbells on the front.

And just this past Thursday, Dana and Mark had brought in their class art project. The companion pieces they'd created took Reeny's breath away. Both of them were composed of four images, each set in its own block of space. Dana's was titled *The Heart's Cry* and her images were of a child crying over a scraped knee, a defeated-looking woman with a letter clutched to her heart, a young man with his hands stuffed in his pockets and kicking at a rock, and an older woman staring down at a headstone. In the bottom corner of each square was a musical note, laying on its side and broken in half. The figures were sketched with an economy of ink strokes, but Dana had done a gut-wrenching job of evoking pain and isolation in each of the frames. She'd obviously poured a lot of her real-life emotion into her work.

Mark's painting was the flip side. It was titled *The Heart's Song* and his blocks contained each of the same people, drawn with the same pen-and-ink medium.

But in his composition, the little girl was laughing as a ladybug crawled on her hand, the young woman was smiling as she read a book to a mostly out-of-frame figure with gnarled hands, the young man was playing catch, again with someone out-of-frame, and the older woman smiled as she held a swaddled infant.

Mark's drawing also contained a musical note in the corner of each square, but it was whole, standing upright and paired with another. Where Dana's drawing embodied alone-ness, Mark's depicted connection.

The images still swirled in Reeny's mind, the shades of meaning changing every time she thought about them.

But the dearest thing that had happened was the change for the better in Philip's attitude. Most of it, she knew, was a result of the fire. That night he'd come to her, wanting to assure her that, though he still wished she'd never started the choir, he'd never wished for something so terrible to happen.

Very gradually, the surliness and hostility had eased. Just yesterday she'd seen him converse civilly with Graham. It gave her hope that maybe, at some future time, there might still be a chance for…

She shook her head, forcibly turning her thoughts away from that slippery ground. Yes, Graham had been very attentive to her lately, but there was no reason to believe it would ever go beyond that. She knew he didn't support her decision to pull her funding out of the choir, and there'd been not even so much as the hint of another kiss.

Better to maintain her focus on getting through today. It wasn't as if her plans for the insurance money weren't going to do lots of good, as well. As soon as that check came in she'd see that the new footbridge was fully funded, right down to a little brass plaque proclaiming it the Ray Landry Memorial Footbridge. No one would have to worry about another accident like Ben's occurring again.

If this would ease some of Ray's mother's pain over the loss of her son, then it was a worthy use of the money. She should have seen that before now.

At the sound of the doorbell, Reeny gave her bow tie one final tug then hurried down the hall, calling for the kids as she passed their doorways. It was an hour and a half until showtime but the kids had wanted to arrive early enough to get a look at some of the booths before they went onstage.

And Graham had insisted on having the three of them ride with him.

She pulled open the door and then gave Graham a grin. Even in a crisp white shirt and a flamboyant green bow tie the man looked distinguished.

He returned her grin. "Do I look that bad?"

She laughed. "Not at all." She tugged on her own tie as her two identically clad children made it to the door. "Besides, there's safety in numbers."

When they reached the park, the first people they ran into were her mom and Jake. "Hey, there," Jake said to the kids. "I think I saw Mr. Delarose over in the dunking booth. You want to come watch your Uncle Jake drop him?"

Philip immediately turned to Reeny. "Can we, Mom?"

"All right, but stay with Uncle Jake. And remember, those shirts need to still be snow white when we get up onstage."

"Yes, ma'am."

She gave Jake a stern look.

He raised his hands, palms out "Okay, sis, I got the message. Snow white."

"Don't worry," Reeny's mom said. "I'll keep an eye on them and get them to the pavilion on time. Y'all go on and check on the choir if you want to."

"Thanks."

Graham put his hand at the small of Reeny's back. "You heard the lady, let's go. I know you're dying to check up on things."

As they strolled down the walkway toward the pavilion, Reeny allowed herself to enjoy the possessive feel of Graham's hand on her back. Even if he was just being gentlemanly, she could pretend there was more to it.

When they reached the pavilion they found the St. Luke's Choir just taking the stage. But Reeny could see the Ding-a-lings' green-clad tables set up along the back of the pavilion.

"Hey, Mrs. Landry."

Reeny turned. "Hi, Jeff. Y'all did a good job getting the tables set up."

"Thanks, but I had lots of help and it didn't take much time at all." He rubbed the back of his neck, then squared his shoulders. "I'm not good with fancy words or anything, but I just wanted to say thank-you—for getting this choir together, I mean. Mark, well, he's got a lot going on with schoolwork and everything, and I figure next year he'll be headed off to college and then moving off who knows where. It's been really nice carving out this time for us to do something together. At least I have a few more months of this to look forward to before he heads out."

He shoved his hands in his pocket. "Anyway, I never got a chance to tell Coach how much I appreciated what he did for me, and I didn't want to make the same mistake with you."

Reeny was caught off guard by his words. She'd had no idea this meant more to Jeff than a way to repay a debt he thought he owed Ray. And before she could get out more than a simple "you're welcome," Jeff had slipped back into the crowd.

She turned to Graham. "That was unexpected."

"Nice to hear, though, wasn't it?"

Dana, who'd been passing by with a chattering group of teenagers, disengaged herself from her friends and ran up to Graham and Reeny. "This is really great, in a totally Ward Cleaver retro kind of way. Who would have thought a little map dot like Tippanyville could put on such a good show?"

Reeny grinned at the girl's enthusiasm. She was a far cry from the withdrawn teenager who'd joined the group two months ago. "Glad you're enjoying yourself."

"Absolutely. Anyway, I just wanted to tell you that I know I was a total grump back when we first got started and that I'm so glad you didn't give up on me. This whole choir is like a second family—full of crazy aunts and awesome cousins that I get to visit with twice a week. And the hand-bells are totally cool. Some of the kids at school have been way impressed that I know how to ring them."

To Reeny's surprise, the girl leaned forward and gave her

a quick hug. "Thanks." Then she raced off to rejoin her friends.

Reeny laughed. "Do you think I'm one of the crazy aunts or an awesome cousin?"

Graham grinned then said self-righteously, "I wouldn't even hazard a guess. I only know which category I fall in."

Reeny shook her head. "True, you just don't fit the 'crazy aunt' mold."

As they began to stroll back toward the area where the booths were set up, Reeny kept puzzling over the unexpected thanks. It made her coming announcement feel like that much more of a betrayal.

She caught sight of Ada and Clotile eyeing some handiwork at a craft booth. "Hey, ladies. What time do you do your number today? I want to make sure I don't miss it."

"We're on at one-thirty," Clotile answered. "We have a really fun program prepared this year."

"If it's half as good as the show you put on at Labor Day, it'll be a crowd-pleaser," Graham responded.

"Why thank you, kind sir." Ada executed a coy curtsey. Then she turned to Reeny. "By the way, you're really making the Glory Be's proud what with all the lives you're touching with this handbell choir. You've accomplished more in two short months than we usually do in a year."

"Oh Miss Ada, you know it doesn't work that way. All our ministries serve a common purpose."

Ada nodded. "All the same, I see God doing a mighty work through you. Just keep it up, young lady."

When they'd moved on, Reeny rounded on Graham. "All right. Just what's going on here?"

He gave her an oh-so-innocent stare. "What do you mean?"

"You know *exactly* what I mean. I find it hard to believe that all of these people just suddenly decided on the same day to tell me what a wonderful job I'm doing."

"I don't. You *are* doing a wonderful job."

"Did you or did you not tell them about my stepping down and redirecting the money?"

He steered her out of the thickest of the foot traffic. "I did not." Then he amended his statement. "Well, I did tell Joscelyn that you were thinking about stepping down."

"I knew it."

He held up a hand. "But I promise I did not say anything about the money and I did not mention any of this to anyone else."

"Then what?"

"All right. I did tell the group that if they had anything they thought they might want to thank you for, then it would be good for you to hear it."

Reeny groaned.

"But I left the *what* and the *when* and even the *if* entirely up to them. And you can't tell me those thank-yous sounded anything but genuine."

She didn't answer right away and he took both her hands in his. "Reeny, can't you see how much the choir members need for it to continue? How much *you* need for it to continue?"

What about you, she wanted to ask. Do you need it to continue, too?

Graham looked past her shoulder, just as she heard a voice hail her name. What now?

Turning, she saw Lavinia had stepped up behind her.

"If you have a minute," her mother-in-law said, "I have something I want to say to you."

Graham started to excuse himself, but Lavinia stopped him. "I don't mind if you hear this, too."

Lavinia stepped forward and took both of Reeny's hands in hers, just as Graham had earlier. "Ever since the fire, I've been taking a long hard look at myself and I haven't liked what I've seen. I'm sorry I made this so difficult for you. I was only thinking about my own feelings. I've been talking to some of your choir members and it really opened my eyes. I think I understand now what it is you're trying to accomplish. And you're right, my Ray would have wanted this so much more than a footbridge."

She studied Lavinia's face, looking for some sign of ambivalence. "Are you sure?"

Ray's mom gave her hands a squeeze. "I can't think of a better memorial for my boy than one that lives and breathes and spreads joy. I'll think of him every time I hear you play. Which I hope will be often."

Reeny felt the murky, suffocating wall that had gone up around her at the news of Ben's accident begin to dissolve. She hugged her mother-in-law for the first time in months and it felt so good.

When she finally stepped back, Graham took her arm, a smile playing on his lips. "Well, Madame Choir Director, we'd best start making our way back to the pavilion."

Lavinia waved them on. "Y'all go on ahead. I need to go find Woody. But we'll be there before the Ding-a-lings start."

As they began walking Reeny turned to Graham. "I was acting pretty selfish, wasn't I?"

"Let's just call it temporarily confused."

She giggled, feeling suddenly lighthearted. "I thought you were fixing to say 'temporarily insane.'"

"That, too."

She gave his arm a playful punch.

"Hey, sis, this guy bothering you?" Jake had come up behind them, closely followed by her mom and the kids.

"Nothing I can't handle."

Philip trotted up alongside her. "Mom, I forgot to tell you but Mr. Lockwood asked if he could ride to church with us tomorrow. I told him he could, okay?"

Reeny felt her gaze widen. Philip actually *wanted* Graham to be with them. "Oh, yes, I think that's an absolutely wonderful idea."

Then she took in the full import of Philip's words and her gaze flew from her son's to Graham's, trying to take in what this meant. Graham had actually asked to join them for *church service*.

She stopped dead in her tracks, causing Jake to almost plow into her.

"Hey, give a guy fair warning."

"Sorry, Jake." Her gaze never left Graham's. "Escort Mom and the kids to the pavilion, please. I need a word with my assistant director in private."

"Sure thing." There was a hint of laughter in her brother's voice, but Reeny ignored it. She had something more important to tend to.

She finally took her gaze from Graham's long enough to have a quick look around. She spied a large half-empty tent situated nearby.

"Come with me." Without bothering to check if he was following, Reeny marched to the far side of the tent. It backed up to a bit of marshy ground though there was solid enough footing if you didn't venture too far. Perfect. No one would interrupt them here.

She turned to find him right on her heels.

"What's the matter?" he asked. "Don't you want me to go to church with you?"

"Of course I do, but only if it's for the right reason." *Please, please, don't say you're just doing this for me.*

He reached up and brushed a lock of hair from her face and it was all she could do not to lean into his touch.

"Reeny, I'd do a lot of things for you, but playing the hypocrite is not one of them. I've been doing lots of soul-searching these past few weeks. Even went in and talked to that pastor of yours. God and I are definitely back on speaking terms."

He'd found his way back to God! "Oh, Graham, this is better than everything else that's happened today." But what had he meant when he said "I'd do a lot of things for you"?

He stepped closer and lifted her chin with his finger. "Reeny, I've fallen quite completely in love with you. And unless you tell me not to, sweetheart, I'm *fixing to* give you the kiss I've been saving for you for four very long weeks."

Then he leaned in and did just that. And it was every bit as wonderful as she'd known it would be. She put her arms around his neck, and with every fiber of her being, she kissed him back, pouring all the love and joy and faith that he'd given her these past weeks right back out to him.

He pulled back, and she was pleased to see that some of his much-prized control seemed a bit shaken. "You, grand master ding-a-ling," he said offering her his arm, "have a choir to direct." Then he gave her a wink. "But afterward, I expect us to continue this very pleasant conversation."

As Reeny strolled toward the pavilion on his arm, she thought of the picture Mark had crafted, and felt her own Heart's Song ring out for all the world to hear.

* * * * *

Dear Reader,

Thank you so much for taking the time to read Reeny and Graham's story. This is my very first foray into writing a story that takes place in contemporary times and hopefully it won't be my last. The setting, too, was a departure from my usual. But I've lived in both southern and northern Louisiana and can attest to the fact that they are two very different and altogether unique cultures. It was fun to set this story in a town that sits somewhere in the middle and is a mix of both.

I've always enjoyed handbell music—not just listening to the wonderful sound of it, but also watching the movements that are like a very precise and well-choreographed dance. It was a real joy to be able to include one in this work.

I love to hear from readers and would be particularly interested in hearing what you think of this particular book. If you've a mind to comment, please contact me via e-mail at winnie@winniegriggs.com, or you can write to me at P.O. Box 14, Plain Dealing, LA 71064.

Wishing you love and blessings,

Winnie

QUESTIONS FOR DISCUSSION

1. Reeny and Graham dealt with their losses very differently. Reeny turned to God and drew comfort and strength from her relationship with Him. Graham felt betrayed and turned away from God. Do you think Reeny's faith was stronger? Why or why not?

2. Reeny decided to spend the memorial money on a handbell choir rather than a more traditional memorial project. What do you think her true motivation for this was? Do you agree or disagree with her reasoning?

3. Graham was insistent that Reeny take the lead role in directing the choir. Given his experience as a choir director, do you feel that was selfish or for the best? Why or why not?

4. Did Reeny's choice of a name for the choir seem silly to you or fun and upbeat? Do you think her mother-in-law was justified in being upset by it?

5. Graham bonded with Reeny's daughter rather quickly. Did this seem believable to you?

6. Did Graham's initial assessment of Reeny as a YOG (someone who justified her busybody tendencies by claiming it was for *Your Own Good*) seem on the nose or a misperception?

7. At what point in the story did you see Graham start to reassess his relationship with God? Did you find his change believable and in character for him?

8. Was Philip's reaction to seeing his mom almost kiss his math teacher believable for an eleven-year-old boy? Do

you think Reeny handled the situation properly or should she have done something different?

9. Reeny was able to roll with the punches through all the problems with starting up the choir, with her relationship with Graham, with the other choir members and even with the fire disaster. However she crumbled when the accident in the park happened. Why do you think this one got to her?

10. Given Lavinia's actions and statements throughout the book, was her about-face at the end believable?

Love Inspired

TITLES AVAILABLE NEXT MONTH

Available June 29, 2010

THE GUARDIAN'S HONOR
The Bodine Family
Marta Perry

KLONDIKE HERO
Alaskan Bride Rush
Jillian Hart

HEART OF A COWBOY
Helping Hands Homeschooling
Margaret Daley

CATTLEMAN'S COURTSHIP
Carolyne Aarsen

WAITING OUT THE STORM
Ruth Logan Herne

BRIDE IN TRAINING
Gail Gaymer Martin

LICNM0610

HARLEQUIN®

A *Romance*

FOR EVERY MOOD™

Spotlight on
Heart & Home

Heartwarming romances
where love can happen
right when you least expect it.

See the next page to enjoy a sneak peek
from Silhouette Special Edition®,
a Heart and Home series.

Introducing McFARLANE'S PERFECT BRIDE
by USA TODAY bestselling author Christine Rimmer,
from Silhouette Special Edition®.

Entranced. Captivated. Enchanted.

Connor sat across the table from Tori Jones and couldn't help thinking that those words exactly described what effect the small-town schoolteacher had on him. He might as well stop trying to tell himself he wasn't interested. He was powerfully drawn to her.

Clearly, he should have dated more when he was younger.

There had been a couple of other women since Jennifer had walked out on him. But he had never been entranced. Or captivated. Or enchanted.

Until now.

He wanted her—*her,* Tori Jones, in particular. Not just someone suitably attractive and well-bred, as Jennifer had been. Not just someone sophisticated, sexually exciting and discreet, which pretty much described the two women he'd dated after his marriage crashed and burned.

It came to him that he…he *liked* this woman. And that was new to him. He liked her quick wit, her wisdom and her big heart. He liked the passion in her voice when she talked about things she believed in.

He liked *her.* And suddenly it mattered all out of proportion that she might like him, too.

Was he losing it? He couldn't help but wonder. Was he cracking under the strain—of the soured economy, the McFarlane House setbacks, his divorce, the scary changes in his son? Of the changes he'd decided he needed to make in his life and himself?

Strangely, right then, on his first date with Tori Jones, he didn't care if he just might be going over the edge. He was having a great time—having *fun,* of all things—and he didn't want it to end.

Is Connor finally able to admit his feelings to Tori, and are they reciprocated?
Find out in McFARLANE'S PERFECT BRIDE
by USA TODAY *bestselling author Christine Rimmer.*
Available July 2010,
only from Silhouette Special Edition®.

HARLEQUIN®

Super Romance®

Top author
Janice Kay Johnson

*brings readers a heartwarming
small-town story*

with

CHARLOTTE'S
HOMECOMING

After their father is badly injured on the farm,
Faith Russell calls her estranged twin sister,
Charlotte, to return to the small rural town she
escaped so many years ago. When Charlotte
falls for Gray Van Dusen, the handsome town
mayor, her feelings of home begin to change.
As the relationship grows, will Charlotte
finally realize that there is no better place
than *home?*

*Available in July
wherever books are sold.*